CRUEL WOMEN, STUPID MEN

A Novel
by
Dan Roentsch

Copyright © 2010 Dan Roentsch
All rights reserved.

ISBN: 1451519095
ISBN 13: 9781451519099

Foreword by Mick Arran

Although you might not think so, genuine literary innovation isn't all that common. In fact, one could argue that since Dickens invented the serial novel almost two hundred years ago, no really original formats have appeared in fiction. Sure enough, there has been a lot of experimentation with styles, starting with Herman Melville and running through William Faulkner, Ferdinand Celine, and EL Doctorow, among others, but there has been precious little in the way of new methods of presenting a written story. The chapter-verse format remains dominant in fiction as it has since Cervantes, and even stylistic pioneering like Truman Capote's "non-fiction novel" or Kerouac's blistering "stream of consciousness" marathons didn't abandon it. Kerouac may have stretched the envelope to the breaking point, but he never succeeded in escaping it completely.

Neither has Dan Roentsch, exactly. What he has done is seize on a new form that was never intended for fiction and adapt it in order to create a brand-new literary form that may change forever the way we look at how stories can be told. If Dan hasn't escaped the envelope, he's certainly found a new shape for it. And it works.

Cruel Women, Stupid Men made its first appearance on the Internet masquerading as a blog. In order to understand just how revolutionary LumpenBlog (its Internet title) was, you first have to know what blogs are. Those of you who do have my permission to skip ahead while I explain them to the rest of the class.

"Blog," kids, is short for "weblog" or "web log." They are online (on the Internet, or "Web") diaries or journals (that's the "log" part, as in, "Captain's Log, Star Date 43-09-69") kept by excessive obsessive/compulsives who think they're writers or believe they have something to say that should be shared with the rest of the world, or both. Blogs began when the Internet geeks who peopled online bulletin boards, news groups, and chat rooms decided that rather than the back-and-forth, tit-for-tat battles of those venues, they wanted a place where they could say what they wanted to say and the people who wanted to read it could find it without having to wade through pages of critiques and counter-opinions.

But the real engine for the spread of blogs was 9/11 and the Afghan War. That's when Internet geeks lost control of the Web forever. Antiwar thinkers, protesters, and activists were frozen out of expressing their opinions in the more usual ways and seized on blogs as if they were electronic pamphlets, New Age cousins to the political flyers and broadsheets of the past. Some of these blogs began to attract the attention of the mainstream media and—more significantly—teenagers. Before you could say, "Get a life," the idea of blogs had been whisked from the hands of political junkies alone and spread like typhoid through the ranks of Internet society. Within a year, there were groups of blogs not just about politics and current events but about everything—from model airplanes and medical waste to baby diapers and trash compactors (items not entirely unrelated, one must confess). It seemed as though everybody wanted to talk to everybody else about everything, and having your own blog was the way to do it.

Then, even the subject-driven bloggers were forced to give way, this time to a legion of me-driven bloggers: the millions upon millions (there were some three hundred million blogs worldwide last time I checked, and since they're breeding like gerbils, we can safely assume there will be twice that number by the time you read this) who signed up for free blogs in order to tell the world what they had for breakfast and what color shoelaces they like. This diabolical and positively ominous development—blogs as daily personal memoirs—is important to note here because therein lies the genesis of LumpenBlog's satire and Dan Roentsch's genius.

Dan recognized earlier than anyone else that the blog format offered a unique opportunity to break the bounds of chapter-verse limitations, especially those of the narrative voice. If you can bear it, think back to your high school English classes. Remember catchphrases like "subjective voice" and "omniscient narrator"? You probably caught them in between naps even if you didn't understand them. A "subjective voice" is fiction written in the first person—"I"—in which everything is presumed to be happening or to have happened in the life of the storyteller. The "omniscient narrator," by contrast, is fiction written in the third person—"he, she, it"—by a narrator who stands outside the story and tells you the thoughts, feelings, and actions of all the characters as if s/he were God and everything s/he's describing is happening to other people.

The limitations of these two voices should be apparent: either you tell everything through the subjective viewpoint of a single character or you tell every viewpoint from the perspective of distance and lose the subjective realities of all your characters by subsuming them in a single narrative voice. These structural limitations have plagued fiction writers for generations, and many have tried to solve it in different ways.

My favorite is the Rashomon-style: tell the story not once through one voice but five times through five different voices and from five different perspectives. In the hands of a Master, this approach can yield remarkable results, but it has proved to be a bit hard on readers. They get sort of fuzzy and blank round about the third version of the same events. They tend to appreciate the novelty of the Rashomon-style the first time they read it and avoid it forever after. Publishers consider that a drawback.

A more successful approach is the multi-narrator style, in which different parts of the story are told by different characters. Lots of writers have tried this one, and while it's more popular with readers than Rashomon, it can still get on their nerves. Every time the writer switches narrators, readers have to get used to a whole new voice and perspective. Each switch necessitates a period of readjustment, of realigning their thought processes and learning to know—sometimes intimately—a whole new person every couple of hundred pages. When it isn't disconcerting, it's utterly confusing. Publishers don't care for that, either.

What Dan saw in blogs that nobody else did was their potential to a) train readers to accept multi-narrators as a storytelling device, and b) give the multi-narrator structure a framework that minimized the confusion and even explained it. Give each character his/her own blog, or better yet, make them participants in a group blog (a blog with entries written by more than one writer), and the multi-narrator style is no longer a mere literary device but an essential component of the narrative itself. It solves the problems of multi-narration very neatly, and readers are enlightened rather than confused. Publishers are generally in favor of enlightened, happy readers.

But I don't want to leave you with the impression that *Cruel Women, Stupid Men* is just a successful literary exercise or that Dan is some kind of latter-day Ponce-de-Leon, exploring new territory to no legitimate purpose. *Cruel Women, Stupid Men* is more than a literary trick. It's a very funny, very sharp satire on everything from the childish, ivory-tower naivety of academia and the perpetual adolescents who populate it, to twenty-first century attitudes toward sex and the power struggle between the genders that has been the storyteller's meat and drink since at least Chaucer, or even—if you wanted to stretch the point—Aristophanes.

LumpenBlog is the group blog of three professors connected with the fictional Belverton University and a project of the BelvU Press, which exists mainly to publish at great expense and minimum sales the academic work of the same three professors. What begins as a new hope for furthering their careers quickly devolves (as do many blogs, I might add) into the arrogant, self-important, and self-referential egotism of the worst of the personal blogs. Pointless and seemingly endless intellectual reflections on generalized and abstract concepts of things like "society" and "relationships" are fairly quickly replaced by the whining of frustrated and half-formed personalities immersed in the trivia of their everyday lives (if sex can be considered trivial, which at my age it can be, thank god).

There is a lot of sex in *Cruel Women, Stupid Men*. All three primary characters and most if not all of the secondary characters are obsessed with it. There's Barry Fest, the purest intellectual of the group, whose pathetic ignorance of all physical activity and the joys thereof, whether of sex or anything else involving muscles not found above the neck, leaves him mystified by the hankerings of the women who have him in their sights. At the same time, he is hypnotized by them, drawn to them, bamboozled by them. Even though he can't bring himself to name particular female body parts (you know the ones, don't make me say them), he wonders about them, dreams about them, fantasizes about them, and craves them.

Barry is your classic, clueless ivory-tower academic. Surrounded by beauty, he pigeonholes it. Faced with complexity, he writes a memo about it. As vain as he is, he is capable of discussing in a calm, level voice his seduction by a much younger woman without realizing that's what it is. The mysteries of a woman's body elude him mainly because he doesn't know there are any. When he is introduced to them in what one must perforce call "extensive practical training" (not so much hands-on as mouth-on, if you get my drift), he doesn't make the connection.

Desmond Cork is Barry's polar opposite. He is BelvU's Rock Prof and a shining example of what happens to failed rockers who go into academia. He calls people "cats" (he calls his girlfriend "the Babecat") and writes dense prose laden with "hep-talk" about rock bands nobody has ever heard of (or ever will). His understanding of even the most superficial music is, well, superficial.

His personal life isn't much better. He's always breaking up with the Babecat, and he has a sort of war on against the Power of Estrogen, to which he seems to ascribe all the evils of the world. Where Barry is pure intellect totally cut off from, let us say, female physical realities, Des is so obsessed with them that he's come to see them as the ultimate threat to the pure masculinity he imagines he represents. If Des has a fictional predecessor, I think it would pretty much have to be Gen. Jack D Ripper in Stanley Kubrick's Dr. Strangelove and his obsession with "precious bodily fluids"—imagine Ripper cross-stitched to a lace bedcover next to Marilyn Manson, and that's Des. He guards his PBFs by evading the Babecat's increasingly frustrated advances and answering his fan mail, forcing the Babecat to seek, um, greener pastures, as it were.

Nefertiti Snorkjutt, the third member of the triumvirate, is Desmond's worst nightmare, a proto-crypto-feminist. Snorkjutt is very concerned about weak women being dragged into the clutches of the brutal male and belongs to Misogyny Watch, whose purpose is to rescue such unlucky women and return them to the, er, fold (many folds, really) of female companionship. The lengths to which Nefertiti will go to rescue women who have succumbed to the power of raw, well, rampant masculinity include twenty-four-hour surveillance, kidnapping, and forced if, uh, loving imprisonment. Like the de-programmers of an earlier era, Snorkjutt sees her duty and does it—over and over until the subject collapses with joy and exhaustion.

I don't want to spoil the many surprises Dan has up his sleeve for you, but if you can resist the temptations of a story that involves training balls, pungent secretaries with loose morals, an interlude with a sort of snake, and an ending in which fellatio and a Zeppelin figure prominently (not necessarily in that order), you're a better man than I am, Gunga Din.

Mick Arran
Boston, more or less

WE START AT LAST
by Barry Fest—*January 5*

Welcome, friends. My name is Barry Fest, and I am the executive editor of the Belverton University Press.

The life of the executive editor at an academic press is a joyous one. I myself write and publish essays on virtually any subject that strikes my fancy. My colleagues, on the other hand, are specialists.

First there is Nefertiti Snorkjutt, who teaches Human Chattel Studies here at Belverton U. I have heard it rumored among the unenlightened that Ms. Snorkjutt is a part-time dominatrix. Permit me to dispute this malicious gossip. Ms. Snorkjutt is simply a committed feminist with a particular interest in reforming misogynists. Yes, she often has to strap them into a chair in order to reform them, and yes, many of them voluntarily return to be reformed—sometimes as often as three times a week—but I do not judge her means. If, in the end, we have a good and agreeable citizen where a bigot used to stand, I say: *well done.*

Then there is Desmond Cork, our resident rock scholar. I have heard it rumored—in those same benighted quarters on the quad—that Desmond is, shall we say, less than exhaustive in his research. Indeed, I have received anonymous phone calls reporting that his version of rock history is entirely made up. Well, Desmond is certainly innovative. And his theory that women in the music industry are driven by the chemical estrogen to make sex slaves of male rock stars is not a popular one. But will you condemn him for this out of hand? Did you condemn Woodward and Bernstein, the journalistic heroes of Watergate fame, for reporting corruption in high office?

I say it is quite possible that we will one day find Desmond's theory to be true after all. And on that day, when estrogen is finally abolished and women are rehabilitated, we will owe Desmond a debt of thanks. And some of you, I daresay, will owe him an apology.

I said earlier that the life of the executive editor at an academic press can be a joyous one. It can also be exasperating. Acquiring publicity for our labors is nigh unto impossible, and acquiring adequate distribution of our printed works has become more difficult with each passing year.

But at last the Belverton University Press is on the Internet. And out here in cyberspace it appears we have more readers than I ever expected, anticipated, nay, *imagined*. Indeed, I am stunned by the size of our readership. The day before our Web site "launched," I went to the room where the computer morlocks keep out of sight—a room that reeks of wire and sharp metal edges—and asked the chief morlock how many visitors we would have on our first day.

He stared at me for a moment as he consumed, inelegantly, a box of Chinese noodles.

"I don't know how many visitors you'll get," he gurgled. "And stop calling me 'morlock.' My name is Todd."

"Well, Todd," I ventured, "the term *morlock* is something of a compliment. It means, roughly, 'unsung hero.'"

"Bull," he said. He wiped his mouth on a napkin and tossed his empty noodle box in the basket by his desk.

"Well, can you give me *some* idea of how many people will read my first words?" I asked.

He took a moment, then said calmly, "I don't know, Fest. Look, you have a hundred gig of bandwidth, that's all I can tell you."

Well, that was something. I seized on it.

"Explain what that means," I said.

"Oh my God. Are you sure?"

"Indeed."

"You better sit down."

I looked at my watch. "No, no, not possible," I said. "Can't you explain it to me in plain English in thirty seconds or less?"

He said nothing, but gave me one of those withering stares for which morlocks, worldwide, have become renown.

So I sat down.

What followed from Todd was a jumble of words and images etched in marker on the whiteboard behind his desk. Lines, circles, a picture of a pipe, the number 1024 over and over…and over!

"So are we good?" he asked finally, taking his seat again.

"Um…yes…so the *width*…" I looked at him steadily so that I might correct myself at the first arched eyebrow, "of the…"

"Pipe."

"*Pipe*…is very…"

"Wide," he said. "It's a very *wide pipe*."

"And it's called *bandwidth*," I started again, "because many…*bands*…can fit in a wide pipe?"

He stared at me for a moment, the fluorescent lights giving his gills a tinge of green. He placed his elbows on his desk, leaned on them, and gently bounced his clenched fists off his lips. Then suddenly his countenance brightened. He smiled. He was almost childlike.

"Yeah!" he said cheerfully, showing me his teeth. "It's because many bands can fit in a wide pipe!"

"Excellent …" I said. I thanked him for his time and started out.

Then I turned to him again. "Say...um..."

"Todd."

"Todd, how many visitors to a band?"

I thought I saw his gills go green again, but then the boyish smile returned, along with the teeth. "About five!" he beamed.

"Superb ..." I thanked him again and returned to the human wing of the building.

Once in my office my mind raced with the math. It was 1024 by 1024...how many times?

I got out my solar powered calculator with the large keypad and placed it under an electric light.

Five times hmmmmm...times hmmmmm...

Oh my God. Thanks to the miracle of modern science, the Internet would deliver over a billion readers to our cybernetic threshold!

I pushed open the French doors (the offices of the Press are in an old townhouse) and walked out onto the balcony. I could see the quad, the gold domes of the university, the dormitories, the glass-and-steel buildings of the city beyond. It was only Belverton, but I had the sense that I was gazing on all the cities of the world from a mystical promontory.

I reached my arms up and clenched my fists in the moist morning air, as if—at last—taking the reins of communication with my public...my *billion*.

I know that many of you will be skeptical. You will say: "But, Fest, a billion is hardly the globe. It is not even the population of India. It is less than a quarter of Asia; less than a sixth of the world! Of what, precisely, are you 'taking the reins'?"

Granted, my friends, granted. A billion is not the globe, but it is a start...a *foothold*, if you will. Truth be told, I would have been happy with a mere million daily visitors. So, I submit, in light of my expectations, my exuberance over a single billion is more forgivable.

Yes, friends, I was exuberant, but then my mood turned bitter. After all, it has long been my contention that the megalomedia has been downplaying the popularity of the alternative and university press, and now I had the numbers from Todd the morlock—a man as dull as a forestry major to the cabals of the humanities—and I was staggered.

I think that you, too, are perhaps sitting there, thinking you are all alone in a world that feeds Madison Avenue while leaving rock scholars destitute and professors of Human Chattel Studies without a lectern. Well, heed my words. We are *not* alone. There are a billion waiting to hear from us.

Of course, I am certain that some of you reading this are not of my mind. Well, I am a tolerant man. I expect the positions, notes, and squibs posted here to be the objects of some debate in our society, even if Big Media keeps them off the television screens. Debate, I submit, is good. And we at Belverton University encourage it. Of course, if we get a lot of fluff from students and teacher's assistants, that would not be good. In fact, Belverton students would be advised to keep their ill-considered opinions to themselves. I am told by Todd that he can track students down over the Internet. And should you give us cause to so trace you, be warned that we will circulate your last name, make funny rhymes with it, and use it in snarky metaphors.

Good reading!

HUMAN CHATTEL STUDIES
by Nefertiti Snorkjutt—January 6

A billion visitors. Well, I suppose that's a good place to, well, I suppose that's a good *start*.

Apparently, several readers were *intrigued* (I suppose that's the right word) by Barry's mention of Human Chattel Studies. Since that course is mine at Belverton, all of the written… well, *email* about it is forwarded to me.

Unfortunately, even a futur—, well, *progressive* school like Belverton University has enough of, how shall I say it? The patriarchal…*influence* that we are unable to offer a degree in HCS. That will change one day, however. How distant that day is depends on how long it takes certain old men to die off, why don't you.

Human Chattel Studies examines such topics as:
- The infamous turtleneck, a well-known symbol for chattel decapitation
- The use of names like "Mrs. Cleaver" in situation… *comedies*—a very obvious attempt to scare chattel with a tool of decapitation.
- The value placed by the patriarchy on good posture, forcing ladies to stand straight and elongate their necks, reminding them how vulnerable they are to decapitation.

- The abbreviation of "decaf" for "decaffeinated." "Decaf" is only one letter away from "decap."
- Government-mandated, universal cunnilingus.

Although Human Chattel Studies is famous locally for its extracurricular activities, there will be fewer of those planned for this year than there were in the, um, *last* year. I am trying to, well, I suppose the phrase is *kick-start* my second career as a television writer. And that is consum—well, *taking up* a lot of my time.

ROCK SCHOLARSHIP
by Desmond Cork—January 8

Lola's a dude. It's true, cats. At least I'm pretty sold on it. See rock scholarship (my specialty here at ye ol' Press) demands an open mind and sometimes when your mind is open? A whole lot of nasty can fly in.

I got reminded that Lola is probably a dude when a cat from Soho in NYC wrote me about it. Here's what he said:

> Hey Des!
>
> I gotta question for ya, babe. Ya know that really terrific song "Lola" that the Kinks did? Ya know the one I mean, right? Hey, ya can't beat the Kinks, can ya? No ya can't! Well, I found out last night that Lola's a guy, dude!
>
> Hey, I got kind of drunk last night at this club. One of the regular girls there is like a DJ, right? So what she does…So what she *does* is she puts on this "Lola" song and we're all dancing and when it's over she says in this dark brown voice, "I hope y'all know Lola is a man."

I almost puked when I heard that, right? But there it was in the lyrics: "I know what I am, I'm a heckuva man, and so's Lola."

What do ya say to that, huh?!
Ernie

Okay time for a breath, cats. That *isn't* how the words really go. See when you're drunk? Words to songs can get *really* jumbled. The words to that "Lola" song though go like this: "I know what I am and I'm *glad* I'm a man, and so's *Lola*."
So if you can brave it out? It *could* mean that *Lola's* glad the *singer* is a man, yeah?
But there's some things about that song that make you have to think that this Lola babe is really just a dude in a dress making guys all steely for a joke or something. Things I cannot overlook without the aid of some delicious Stoli *cum* OJ. See if you're like me you spent a lot of afternoons and some late nights in the hot summer behind the bathroom door thinking about that Lola babe putting you on her knee and saying, "Come home with me." And then your best friend's half-sister Candy who never knocks walks in and kind of chuckles and leaves, and you go out later all nervous and whatnot and you find her in the living room having a Maker's Mark and listening to the Tijuana Brass and patting the sofa next to her like she's been saving the space for you, and you look at her and she looks at you…
So anyway…yeah. Lola. She's a dude, cats.

PERP & VIC: MBU
by Nefertiti Snorkjutt—January 21

Well, I am what I suppose most people would call *thrilled* to announce that I have finally begun my second career as a television writer. This "career" may be short-lived. I scoff at television as a matter of, well, *principle*, and it is hard to convince those for whom you have contempt that they should keep buying your little scripts, you know? Thank God for agents!

I am sure you all know the very popular police drama, *Perp & Vic*, which has been syndicated to virtually, well, perhaps I should not go so far as to say *virtually*, but I suppose nearly *every* television station in existence. My agent has been sending them my gender-sensitive scripts for ages now, and they have never been interested.

Well, at last someone came up with a spin off of the original series. It is called *Perp & Vic: Men Are Bastards Unit*. My agent—Allison Muffplug—immediately phoned me up and, well, the rest is history. My script is not the pilot but will appear in the first season.

The show is about a two-person squad consisting of a square-jawed woman with an uncertain hairstyle and her sensitive-man partner. The producers won't—well, at any rate, I *think* they won't—mind if I provide our billion readers with an excerpt. In this scene, Detective Parkdrive (the woman with the square jaw) and Detective Redhook (her sensitive partner) are sharing a pizza after responding to one of the many calls they get from women around eleven p.m.

> *Redhook*: All right, maybe he isn't as polite to his wife as he is to strangers. I don't know. I'm just saying we have to be sure before we take it to the DA.
>
> *Parkdrive*: I don't know what more you want. We have the word of the delivery boy that he was extremely polite when paying for the duck and egg rolls—
>
> *Redhook*:—tipped big, too—
>
> *Parkdrive*:—but once the door was closed they flicked on the TV set and started watching *The L Word*.
>
> *Redhook:* Big mistake. Men should watch *Deadwood*.
>
> *Parkdrive*: Well, there's a gynophobic remark if I ever heard one.
>
> *Redhook*: I'm just saying if men and women don't want to argue they're better off watching gold miners urinate.
>
> *Parkdrive* (*checking her notes*): They were good for a while, and then the wife asked the husband why the short girl with the boyfriend was flirting with the tall woman.

Redhook: Right.

Parkdrive: And he said, "Babe, can you pipe it down? I know as much about this as you."

(*Redhook whistles.*)

Redhook: Tough stuff.

Parkdrive: "Pipe it down," he said.

Redhook: What a Cro-Magnon.

Parkdrive: You mean Neanderthal.

Redhook: I mean jerk. Problem is, we don't have any corroboration. We just have the wife's word.

Parkdrive: And of course, a woman's word isn't good enough. That's about what I'd expect from someone who got kicked out of film school for shooting women's breasts in high-def and calling them *cans*.

Redhook: Hey, that was five years ago. Since then I've learned to hate the word "cans." I throw my garbage in a receptacle and buy my tuna in metal cylinders.

Parkdrive: Yeah, you're a real sport. I'll bet right now you're wearing a bra. With open nipples.

Redhook: Hey look, I want to get this *L Word*-watching bastard as bad as you. I just don't want him getting off on a technicality.

Later, in the denouement, Parkdrive tells Redhook she's sorry she brought up the cans incident. I know, it's hard to believe that a *really* strong woman would be able to stand the sound of her own voice saying "I'm sorry," but they have to work together and it is, after all, *television*.

WMD KIDNEY
by Barry Fest—January 22

I am not what one could reasonably call a superstitious man. However, when I learned from Todd the morlock that our online readership was an approximate billion, I immediately began to dread the worst. The other shoe, to indulge the parlance of certain elderly peasants, would surely drop. Fate would see to it that my good fortune was leavened with grave tidings.

And so it was.

The grave tidings were brought me by my doctor. Nay, not one doctor, but two.

Yes, it now appears obvious to me that while it is extremely difficult for the combined military of several mighty nations to find weapons of mass destruction in Iraq, it is fairly easy for a urologist to find one in a fellow's kidney.

It began last week with a pain. A pain that I shall not, from a sense of delicacy, attempt to describe. I went to see my regular physician, Dr. Norman Hess, whom I normally see once per year for an inglorious inspection made with a rubber glove.

"Let's take you for some scans," he said.

"And where," I eyed him, "will these scans be had?"

He named a respectable hospital. But I know only too well that names are taken in respectable hospitals. Names, DNA, and telephone numbers. Descriptions are noted of the patient's physique, and often these descriptions are sarcastic. A nurse working in such an institution once confided to me the existence of a one-to-ten "doability" scale, which she was required to fill out and sign on each of her male patients.

I refuse to stand for such objectification, so I demanded that Hess find for me a truly private hospital with a truly private privacy policy.

And he did.

On the outskirts of Belverton, high on a hill, is a mansion that was at one time a hotel and casino for runaway slaves traveling the Underground Railroad, and which is, today, St. Catarrh's General Hospital. I was immediately at ease. The doctors on the staff of St. Catarrh's are reputed the most condescending north of the Mason-Dixon line. Nevertheless, on first seeing the ancient manse under a full moon, I expected to hear a voice from an upper room cry "Mother, no! Mother…blood!"

I surmounted these trepidations and succumbed to the scans. My new doctor, a specialist named Frommerheilen, reported back to me.

"I wish I could give you a clean bill of health," he said as he slapped one of my scans over the light box. "But look here, at this blotch. Our analyst believes it is a trailer capable of producing poison gas."

"Hmm," I said. "It would have to be a rather small trailer, would it not?"

"Amazing what they can do with nanotechnology these days."

"How do you think…they got it in there?" I asked.

"Their usual method? Prostate exam."

That bastard Hess!

"So do you want me to take it out or what?" asked Frommerheilen.

I sank into his shiny black office chair with the metal arms.

"Will you place it in a bottle and let me take it home?" I asked. "I think it would make an excellent subject for a monograph."

He agreed.

A few days later, after coming out of the artificial coma that spared me the pain of incision, Frommerheilen stood over my bed, a rusty little trailer rattling in a plastic vial.

"Incredible!" I said, staring.

"And look!" he said. "While we were in there rummaging, we found this!"

He produced another vial, and in this, it seemed, was a jagged shard of…something.

"My God," I said, staring. "May I see it?"

He reluctantly paced the vial in my outstretched hand.

"All right," he frowned. "You can look at it for now. But this afternoon it goes back to the Baghdad Museum."

LOOKING FOR LOLA
by Desmond Cork—January 23

  You know how that babe Lola in the Kinks song called "Lola" is really a dude and whatnot? Well, you can still pretend she's a babe. And if you've got some time and like a pencil? You can make up different words to sing over that part where you find out she's a dude.
  Figuring that out pretty much changed my life, cats. I got this hard crush on the Lola from my version of the song and when I got my own place after my folks said get out I got some posters and whatnot of babes probably not named Lola but who look a lot like I thought she might look and I put them up all over my new apt. Then my best friend's half-sister Candy who came by said I could call her Lola if I did stuff, so I did and that helped, but Candy didn't have the dark brown voice like Lola and even when she tried? She couldn't hug me so tight I thought she'd break my spine, which is also from that song.
  So this one afternoon I decided I would find a babe named Lola for real and I threw on my jeans and my half-boots and this black T-shirt with a skull on one side and a picture of Joey Ramone on the back and went out hunting for Lola 'cause I was pretty sure she would be down with the whole black T-shirt scene with a picture of a Ramone and maybe even the skull.

But before I went out looking I sat down on like the edge of my bed and looked at my half-boots on my feet and said to myself all quiet-like, "Okay dude, don't let this Lola chick know right off that you've been hunting her down or she'll get scared and split and then you'll have to find some other chick named Lola and remember not to scare *her* off."

"Got it," I said.

So I went out and started walking around Belverton where I live and I went down to the Futon District where they have these beatnik cafes that you have to walk down steps to get to. I stopped on the sidewalk in front of ye ol' Board Treaders Theatre on Veblen Street 'cause there was this line outside, cats. Okay, it was a little clumpier than a line? But not as clumpy as a crowd. And it was the middle of the day, which I thought was tray strange because usually people don't hang out there except at night.

I'm about to go off and look for Lola some more when this babe walks kind of zigzaggy through the clumpy line and across the ol' sidewalk toward the street and almost bumps into me, and she has on these kind of jeans that hug a chick's butt really hard so that her butt crack is like the only thing you can think about until you see another one and then maybe even after that. And she had this blonde hair in pigtails and this black guitar case and she was crying, cats.

So she's sort of leaning up against this metal post with the light at the top and she drops the guitar case so the thin part is sort of sticking in the road. I'm kind of walking by in back of her and watching her butt crack because one it's a babe's butt crack and two I'm straight and I think about babes' butt cracks a lot. And the butt this crack is in? It's a *happening* butt.

I had it pretty much memorized so I turned around to go off again when I heard this voice behind me say, "Excuse me. Cat. Got a minute, cat?"

So I stopped and looked at her face this time. She had this smile like she's regular instead of stuck up like some babes are who have happening butts and she says, "Got a tissue I can borrow, cat?"

There was something about the way she talked that I thought was tray cool and I noticed that her eyes were all watery and her nose was starting to run and her voice was gurgly so she definitely needed a tissue bad.

And I said, "I don't have a tissue babe, but I've got a dollar you can use."

And she looked at me all confused-like and said: "A dollar, cat?"

And I'm like, "Yeah and if you let me take you to lunch I have a five you can blow your nose on if you don't feel weird because it has the Lincoln picture and he was tragically shot and all."

She kind of giggles and says she'll have lunch with me even if I don't give her money to blow her nose on and anyway I had one of those tiny packs of tissue in my backpack (oh yeah, I had my backpack with me). So I give her this pack of tissues and she turns around over this big wastebasket the Belverton garbage dudes put on every street corner and starts honking away and wiping her eyes and it took awhile, but when she turned around again she was all smiley and her face was all dry and the tissues? Totally destroyed, cats. And I'm thinking, "Des, if you need a tissue what'll you use?" and then this other part of my brain says, "Use the dollar, dude," and I'm like, "Oh yeah."

So me and this babe go off to lunch. She almost forgot her guitar until I pointed it out and then she sort of picked it up and put it on her shoulder real easy like it was made of paper or something. Then she gave me this look like, "Where to?" I didn't know where stuff was in the Futon District so she named this taco place called Friend Flicka's and she led the way and the whole time we're walking I'm thinking about one her butt crack and two tacos and how tasty those are.

And well, I don't know what words to say a lot of times when I meet somebody? So I'm just saying "bogus" and "whoa" and she's talking about Belverton and how it's a drag living here and how it would probably be better to move to New York or L.A. or someplace where people do stuff.

"Because New York and L.A.?" she says. "Those are *happening* towns, cat."

We get to the driveway at Friend Flicka's when she stops talking and it was quiet for a few seconds and I think, "Whoa, my turn." So I say out loud to her: "Um. Babe. So. You like the ol' tacos, eh?"

And she stops real sudden-like and looks at me and she is *not* smiling, cats. She looks kind of angry or maybe just fed up and says: "Look. Cat. Sometimes a taco is just a taco, cat."

I didn't really know why she said that? But it sounded pretty on the nose. The only thing I could think of to add on was: "Yeah, it's just a taco unless you get it with some of that happening hot sauce and maybe some chili. Then I guess it's still a taco but they call it something different on the big board in front where the cats in the aprons stand."

She gives me this look where she opens her mouth and then sort of closes it. And just when I think she's about to break mad again she smiles real big and says, "You're *different*, cat!"

Then she grabs one of my hands and squeezes it hard and leads me into Friend Flicka's. We get to the ol' table and she puts her guitar down and sits down across from me so no more butt to look at. That's when I ask her, hey, like, why was she crying and all in front of the Board Treaders Theatre on Veblen Street?

And she's like "oh god it's so embarrassing" and I'm like "oh come on tell me." So she tells me she was at the Belverton tryouts for that reality show or contest or whatever called *American Idol* that they have on TV.

Right then the waiter dude shows up and he's wearing a Friend Flicka's cap and he looks kind of sad or maybe just miffed and he takes our order which was pretty much tacos. Then when he goes away the babe says she flunked the ol' *American Idol* tryouts, and that that's pretty bad but what was really harsh was the tryout, cats? They were mean to her because her guitar was way out of tune and so they stopped her before she got to sing words and they were like, "You'll never get anywhere in this biz" and "Whatever so possessed you to come into this here tryout?" and whatnot.

"Hey, babe," I said, "I grok the whole out-of-tune nasty. See, I used to be in a band? And all the cats in it were like hardcore and whatnot but we could *not* tune our guitars, babe. So we got this idea to look for digital guitars that would maybe beep when they got in tune."

And she puts down this glass of water that the waiter dude left and says, "So did you find any, cat?"

"Nope," I told her. "We sort of broke up? But we're saving up for new guitars. It isn't so much that we don't have the money as like they haven't invented digital guitars yet. I froogle for them every night so when they're invented we'll be there with the cake.

"Because this band? It's a *happening* band, babe."

"Well, cat, the reason my guitar was out of tune today was because I *wanted* it to be out of tune."

"Whoa."

"Yeah. Because I was about to sing that 'Lola' song by the Kinks? And you know how at the beginning the guitars are all out of tune and they're like brang, brang, brangity-branky-brang-brang!

"Hey. Cat. You all right, cat?"

I just kept staring at this babe and like for the time that I was staring at her? I forgot all about her butt crack. Which if you're religious or just not real practical is pretty much a sign that you're a good person finally.

So I told her all about how I was looking for Lola from the song "Lola" by the Kinks and how my best friend's half-sister Candy found out by walking in on me when I was busy in the bathroom that time and how she did things with me that like felt good and that she let me call her Lola.

"And like today?" I said. "Today I was out looking for Lola when you bullet-walked through that clumpy line!"

And this babe with the happening butt that I stopped thinking about for a while? She's like: "Cat. That is *not* all, cat. See—"

"I know, babe, the Lola in that song is a dude the way the Kinks sing it. But see, my philosophy on life is why not sing 'Lola' so she ends up being a babe?"

"Cat. What if I told you my name was Lola, cat?"

"I don't know what I would say babe but don't you think it was enough you were about to sing the song?"

I waited for her to answer but she just sort of looked at me with her eyebrows pushed together when the dude with the Friend Flicka's cap comes over with the tacos finally. And while he's putting the tacos down I'm thinking, "Hey, what *would* I say if she told me her name was Lola?" I guess first I'd try to remember not to scare her off by telling her I was hunting down a babe named Lola. But since I already told her I was hunting down a babe named Lola? I guess I would be in kind of a jam, cats.

And right when I'm thinking about it she bites into this taco and she's looking at me with her eyebrows pushed together still and she just bursts out crying again.

And I'm like, "Babe, what, I mean" and stuff and she's like, "Oh, it's been a really bad week" and stuff and I'm like, "Why?" And she says she also lost her job.

"I don't mean to dump it all on you like this," she says, sort of catching her breath and wiping her face off with a napkin. "I can't pay the *rent*…I'm getting *evicted*…"

"Well what happened, babe? Why so disrupt-o?"

"Okay." She sort of sniffled here and then she said: "I'm really into fitness, cat. That's why I have this happening butt you've been staring at since the second you saw me."

"Cool."

"And I used to be a gym teacher at St. Balthazar's School for Girls, and I was also coach of the soccer team."

Right that minute? I'm thinking she could maybe beat me up, cats.

"So the girls on this soccer team and also like the principal and almost all the other teachers they're really into these halftime prayer deals where the whole team gets on their knees and the coach prays out loud to Jesus to let the girls on our team flog the chicks on the other team. Not a real lot? But if the chicks on the other team aren't asking as hard as maybe we are then like, what's in it for Jesus to give them a boost, eh? I mean, if you had nails put in your hands and whatnot for the sins of girls in sports bras you maybe would be thinking about where their energy is when it's their turn to beg for stuff."

(I had a mouthful of taco so I just nodded, cats.)

"So this one game we're out on the field flogging butt, and its seven to one and like it's half time, time to beg the Lord. So the girls get on their knees and I…well, the prayer started out normal I guess, but right about in the middle I pretty much just started to bad-mouth Jesus."

"Whoa. To his face?"

"Yeah…I guess I'd been thinking about some things that bugged me and not saying anything, and then there I was in this prayer and it all just came out. I was like, 'Okay Lord, thanks a load for helping us out. Hey, Lord, if you're really there and whatnot why don't you help the girls on the other team because a lot of them are kind of fat and clumsy and I think that if you really gave a rat's butt you might want to see about getting them in shape so later on they won't just have memories of skinny chicks taking the ball and their boyfriends away. I mean, give thanks to the Lord and all that, but we're winning because we work out and practice and they're losing because they eat pizza and veg on the couch, eh? Maybe they're in their locker room on their bellies right now begging you real good, but they can beg until they ralph on their shoes and we'll still flog lard in the second half because practice means everything and kissing angel butt means squat. Whatcha say to that, Lord? Hello? Hey, Lord, you really should get like one of those roaming plans because wherever you are I don't think you're covered."

I'm just sort of looking at her because she's like the first person I ever met to flame Jesus.

"That next Monday? One of the girls on the team who's real pure and whatnot ratted me out to the principal and he called me in and he was tray mad. And he asked me if I was a Christian and I said I used to think so but I guess maybe not so much anymore and he said, 'Well, you know this is a school with the word "saint" in the name?' And I'm like, 'Yeah,' and he's like, 'Well do you at least believe in Intelligent Design?' And I said I didn't think so because there are a lot of things that are designed hinky. Like men. Have you seen men naked? Especially the parts that get really gross when they chunk out and they can't keep their shirts tucked in? And like skin. If God wanted humans to be in charge like it says then why didn't He design their skin to be harder for bears and whatnot to bite through?"

"Whoa. So what did he say, babe?"

"Well, I was really wanting him to answer? You know to like give me his theory on it? But he was really mad at me so he called up this nun that has to say okay before he can fire people and when she heard it was me she said okay.

"And that aft my boyfriend says he just made his soul mate pregnant and they're going to have the baby and be normal."

"Whoa. Some dude dumped you because you lost your day job? That is *harsh* babe."

"No, he said he was planning to dump me ever since he started throwing his soul mate the bone and I didn't even know he had a soul mate. So then he said I was an animal and that I kept making him do stuff he wasn't really into."

I took a drink of water and looked at my plate. "Hey babe," I said, "I get it about the bad-designed dudes and all, but what about chicks? I would have to say that many chicks are intelligently designed. Especially the really physical ones who work out."

I kept looking at the plate but I could see out of the top of my eyes that she was picking up a napkin and I could hear her giggle. I was sort of nervous that she might have figured out that I was not real into soul mates myself and that might scare her off.

Then I heard her say in this high voice that was kind of shaky: "You can't tell just by looking, cat."

Whoa.

"You also have to taste."

"Taste?" I said. "And where would I taste a babe, babe?"

So she took me home to her apt and showed me, cats. And she showed me the next night too and every night for like a week until I was hooked.

I was lying there Saturday in her bed all shaky like a babe-taste junky and I said, "Hey, um, babe…"

"Cat. You don't have to keep calling me Babecat."

"I didn't call you Babecat."

She sort of giggled and her eyes got big. "You *could* call me Babecat if you want," she said and then she giggled again.

"Okay Babecat," I said. "You wanna move into my place?"

So she did and she's been there ever since.

And like, looking for Lola? Well I decided to give that up if you don't count pretending the Babecat's name is Lola sometimes. A few times I even slipped up and called her Lola out loud and she just played along because the Babecat? She's a *happening* babe.

FEMINIST EYE FOR THE MISOGYNIST GUY
by Nefertiti Snorkjutt—January 26

I think the full lot of—well, *billion* of you probably want to know more about me. Hm. Well, you know about my Human Chattel Studies class, and—oh yes—you know about my avoc—well, *second* career as a television writer.

I think one more thing you should know is that one of my extracurricular projects is Misogyny Watch, which is, well, a *hotline* that women of all ages can call to report on misogynists in their classrooms, offices, and bedrooms. Misogyny Watch keeps a list of reports on all suspected misogynists, and when these reports on a given misogynist reach what you might call *critical mass*, we *swing* into *action*.

A few weeks ago we started getting reports on a fellow named, well, *Bruce*. Here are the reports we received:

- Dec 4—Asked on a date by a strong woman, refuses, asserting: "I need a chick with tattoos."
- Dec 12—Approaches colleague on a Friday night, asks her if she's busy that weekend. On ascertaining her availability, asks: "Can I try out my Cialis refill on ya, babe?"
- Dec 19—A week later, arrives at a young woman's house for what was supposed to be a night of

shimmering romance, and asks: "So, ya really wanna do the dinner thing, or ya wanna start slammin'?"

That, well, was all we needed to know to pay Bruce a call. It was my turn, so I made the visit. When he opened his apartment door he was wearing a day's worth of stubble, a T-shirt that looked like it came right out of the plastic pack, and a pair of tight jeans with a silhouette in the crotch that looked more like Florida than Cape Cod.

"Whaddaya want, babe?" he asked.

I shouldered in and slapped him around a little.

A few weeks of these visits later and he was wearing chinos with enough front space to hide a small monument. He was calling me "Ms. Professor Snorkjutt, ma'am," and even volunteered to rewire my basement game room free of charge, even though he is not an electrician.

Then it got away from me somehow. It seems I'd had, well, a plan to *reform* the misogynist, but not a plan to *keep* him reformed. I walked up to his house one day, and I could hear loud punk rock vibrating the walls from the inside. Worse, the voices singing were female—fem punks providing Bruce with the dangerous illusion that women want sex. When I was leaving that day, I heard his voice behind me say, "Nice shanks," and when I turned to confront him he just smiled with this glint in his eye and said, "Ya wanna stay?"

And, well, I *did*. It *is* a quagmire. In fact, I'm in his bedroom right now, tapping this entry out on my laptop. If anyone out there knows an exit strategy, please email me ASA, well, P.

WHY ARE THERE BAD ROCK BANDS?
by Desmond Cork—February 1

    Hey cats. I get email all the time. Really. And like most of it? It's about my mortgage or from married chicks who want to date me because their husbands are only in the position of being missionaries or something, but some of it is about stuff I'm interested in, like rock scholarship.
    And like one of the things you cats should know about rock scholarship is that it is highly demanding, which is something I'm always telling the Babecat because when I want to do rock scholarship? That's usually when she wants me to drop trou and flash nasty.
    And up until a few weeks ago she always got her way because I was hooked on the taste of pure babe, and when you're a babe-taste junkie? Pretty much everything else goes out the window, cats.
    But then about two weeks ago the Babecat got kind of miffed at me because I suggested that maybe she should put on pants when we know we're about to get a pizza or something. (It was just a suggestion, cats.) She wasn't miffed at me for long? But it was long enough for me to go through babe-taste withdrawal.

So right now the Babecat is in the other room saying, "Des. Dude. Time to strap on the kneepads, dude."—But I got rock scholarship to do, yeah?

Here's one I got today:

> Des Cork,
>
> Hi! My name is Nikki but my friends call me Sayt. We (my friends and me) thought you could answer this question. Is that all right with you?
>
> Anyway, we were just noticing that there's a lot of rock bands that are, oh gosh, I don't want to put anyone down but there are a lot of rock bands that are really *bad.* Have you ever noticed that?
>
> It seems like, well, it just seems like that some people get into rock for the wrong reasons, you know? I mean, at least learn to play an instrument, right? So why is that? Do you have an opinion? I mean, do they all just want the sex or what?
>
> Sayt

Okay, that's a kind of hard question to answer? Because it's different for chick rockers than it is for regular rockers. For the chicks it's all about the sex because estro keeps them baked.

But like most musicians who are dudes? They really don't care about sex. Yeah, there's a lot of groupies and whatnot (estro again cats) but for most guys it's like: "Sorry babe I have a girlfriend, yeah? And like it's a steady deal."

Most cats get into rock because they see these bios of rockers on VH1 so they dream of one day having a bio on

VH1. That means they have to go into rehab to make the bio a good story which means they have to get hooked on drugs or act out like they're junkies so that doctors and nurses say: "Whoa. Junkie." Most rockers are really bad at acting stuff out? So to get into rehab they almost all become real junkies instead.

And like, I used to be in a band? And me and the hardcore cats who used to be in the band, we still have these parties sometimes and talk about the cool stuff we'll do when they invent digital guitars and we can be in a band again. Well, we had one of these parties last week and I took the Babecat and I think that at this party everything you could drink was sexed up, even the tap water. So there we were on this white sofa with coffee stains all over it and I'm like, "Whoa. Babecat. I can smell beige." And she's like, "Des. Cat. I can see alto, cat." And then this cat whose house we were in comes up and he's like, "Des. Lola. Time to like, split."

And he says it a few times and I sort of hear him and this part of my brain is thinking, "Whoa! There's a babe named Lola at this party!" But this other part of my brain thinks it's on the ceiling somewhere. So then I hear him say, "Okay Candy, he's all yours," and I feel someone step up on my lap and then I sort of pass out.

And when I wake up it's like the next day and whatnot and I'm in my best friend's half-sister Candy's bed at her house and my face is all sticky and when I get home the Babecat won't talk to me for like two days.

I think I answered that question you asked? But if I didn't you should shout back and let me know.

LOLA VS. THE MISOGYNIST
by Nefertiti Snorkjutt—February 6

Well, it's been two weeks since I *escaped*—or at least *evaded*—the clutches of Bruce. Thanks to all of you out there who helped me with my, well, *exit strategy*.

When I wrote to you last time, I was trapped in Bruce's bedroom with nothing but a vibrating man and his laptop computer. Fortunately, I was able to reach the laptop from the bed, so I could check my email whenever I got a hand free. I must say that I got some rather, um, *helpful* suggestions. I might have been able to get out without any help at all, except that Bruce is the type of misogynist who knows how to keep one part of woman's body, well, *entertained* while other parts of her body are *resting up*, you know? (Besides, after a while I couldn't remember which room I left my pants in.)

Here's what some of you wrote to me:

> Hi Nef!
>
> How horrible for you! Have you tried kicking him in the crotch?
>
> Erica

Hm. Well, that came to mind. I commanded him to back away and stand up, so that I could get a clean shot, but by the time I had acquir—well, *drawn a bead* on the target I was facing in the other direction.

> prof. snorkjutt:
>
> Okay, I think this works. The next time he's catching his breath, say, "Bruce, we have had some fun times together, and maybe in the future we will have more fun times. But for now I just think that I need something more stable in my life, and I think you should think about whether this is the sort of relationship you want to have with a woman."
>
> sincerely,
> rhonda

Well, this was a very good suggestion, but I kind of, well, *messed it up*. I got up to "maybe in the future we will have some more fun times," but instead I shouted, "To the core, you beautiful bastard! To the core!"

> Nef. Babe. Here's what we'll do, babe. Reply to this email with Bruce's home address. Talk him into turning the lights out. I'll slip in and spell you until you can split.
>
> Lola

That's the one that worked. Lola was there in a jiff—well, *no time*. I put the lights out, claiming modesty, and Bruce… *went* for it. He rolled over after a few moments and Lola slipped in beside him while I slipped out. I found a pair of his chinos in the living room and escaped into the night, leaving my laptop back in his, um, *sex room*.

The next morning it was raining a cold winter rain, but I thought I should risk getting wet to revisit Bruce's apartment to make sure he wasn't harming Lola's dignity—well, not too much, anyway. I knew something was wrong as soon as I stepped out of the elevator on his floor and could see a note in his handwriting taped to his apartment door. Here's what it said:

> Professor Snorkjutt, ma'am:
>
> Lola and me are headed to Maui!
>
> P.S. I took the laptop, so drop us a Gmail sometime!

So I called in some sabbatical time and now I'm off to Maui to rescue Lola. I can more than, well, *imagine* what that poor girl is going through!

MEET MOLIERE
by Barry Fest—February 13

Here at Belverton University we like to think of ourselves as working in the very *vanguard* of modernity. Thus we have committed ourselves to the use of glMail, an email software that detects the sexual orientation of an email's author, marks the email accordingly (e.g., "from Joe Smith—Gay"), and places it in the inbox.

Starting Friday, glMail began to misbehave. A gay friend of mine phoned me up and said he was sending me an email link to a page at BushTush.org, where you can click on a photograph of George W. Bush's face and watch it morph into—yes—a tush.

I waited and waited, but the missive never arrived—or so I thought. Then, whilst rummaging about in the folders, I found that my friend's email had been placed in my outbox instead of my inbox.

Several other missives from several other gay friends received the same treatment. Nothing was wrong with them except that they had been placed in my outbox. Perturbed, I summoned Moliere.

Moliere, I suppose I should tell you, was hired by our chief morlock, Todd, to be our email administrator. She is, I believe it is fair to say, quite an individualist. Her waist-length hair is, in part, twisted into a purple braid, her nails are painted black, her face is pale, her eyes are large. When she entered my office to tend to the glMail problem, she was wearing a skirt that looked like the bottom half of a black wedding dress and a black tank top with the words NEED MEAT BAD in white lettering across the chest. Reaching out from beneath this shirt were the head and appendages of a tattooed dragon, its red tongue licking her nape and green wings sleeving her arm.

She crept in silently, and I did not know she was there until I caught the reflection—in the computer monitor—of her eyes staring at me impatiently. "Ya gonna move, boss?" she asked. "Or ya wanna lap dance?"

I stood up and aside. I am not used to such familiar treatment by morlocks, but for some reason I did not mind at this juncture. The tone of her voice was making me *tingle*, and I endeavored to distract myself by thinking of my wife—Dr. Wharton-Stone. That by itself did not work, so I tried to imagine Dr. Wharton-Stone wearing some lingerie I had recently seen on a bald mannequin.

"So," Moliere said as she tapped the keyboard, "you don't like it in the outbox, huh?"

I mumbled something I do not precisely recall, as I was fascinated, enthralled, nay, *mesmerized* by the size and detail of the dragon tattoo.

"Like the ink?" she asked. Her reflection seemed to smile. I cleared my throat. "Well, why not?" she continued. "You're a growing boy."

She giggled.

I did not want to leave her with the wrong impression. "I was thinking of my wife," I claimed. "She is a professional. She does not have tattoos."

"Well," Moliere said, still tapping keys, "life sucks for you, doesn't it?"

I was appalled by her presumption, but there was that *tingle* again.

"Okay," she said, standing, "it's fixed. You'll get it in the box you want it in."

She went out, and I sat back down in the chair. The seat was warm. My nervous system embraced that heat, friends. Nay, it wrapped its neuronic arms about it, as one might wrap one's arms about an old flame only to find her hands moving non-platonically over one's trousers.

I stood and tried to focus my mind on matters of greater uplift than Moliere's blood heat. Then I foraged through my desk drawer and found one of my wife's business cards. "VICTORIA WHARTON-STONE, MD—Professional Psychotherapist," it said. I circled the word "Professional" and taped the card to my monitor.

The tingling will stop soon.

OFF TO MAUI
by Nefertiti Snorkjutt—*February 27*

Well, it's been a little while, but I am in Maui at last, looking for Bruce and the courageous Lola.

You, um, well, you should remember that Lola was the young lady who rescued me from the carnal acrobatics of Bruce, a misogynist I was in the process of reforming when he made a, well, an *overt* appeal to my biology. Lola stood in for me while I ran to my car, only to have him take her away with him to Maui the next day.

So I am in Maui to rescue her, as I said. I am not one to, well, *refuse* to return a favor. I am not what you might call an *ingrate*.

During the long flight from Belverton to Maui, an idea for an episode of *Perp & Vic: Men are Bastards Unit* seemed to, well, I supposed the word is *pop* into my head from *nowhere*. Creativity is won—well, it's extraor—I mean, it's *unusual*, isn't it? Perhaps I do have a muse, or maybe not a muse, but at least an *elf*.

Anyway, once I had the idea I pitched it to my agent—Allison Muffplug—over the in-flight cell phone and began typing the first ver—well, *draft* on my laptop somewhere over San Diego.

For those of you who do not know the program, *Perp & Vic: MBU* is a crime drama about two detectives: a square-jawed woman named Parkdrive and her *reformed-misogynist* partner, Redhook. They hunt misogyny wherever it rears its ugly, well, *head*.

Here is an excerpt from the teleplay.

Parkdrive swaggers past a holding cell. Redhook tags along behind her. In the holding cell is a thin man with a bad dye job and eyes bloodshot from falling asleep with his contacts in.

Man in holding cell (raving): What happened to the eighties!? Women wanted sex in the eighties! What happened!? Where did they go?!

Redhook: Can you believe that guy? I mean, I can remember I thought the same thing back in my misogynist days. What a crock, right, Parkdrive?

Parkdrive is lost in thought.

Redhook (cont'd): I said it's a crock, right, Parkdrive?

Parkdrive turns and faces him. They both stop walking. She has mist in her eyes.

Parkdrive: I have a confession to make, Redhook.

Redhook: Go on. I'm your partner.

Parkdrive: I…I once enjoyed sex myself.

Redhook tries not to judge.

Parkdrive (cont'd): His name was Bryce. He wore crotch-hugger jeans and he had this way of describing what he was about to do to you that...that...

Redhook: Steady, Parkdrive. Just tell me.

Parkdrive: Well, it went right to a woman's...*biology*.

Redhook (through his teeth): Freaking biology! It's like a voice coming from your...you know.

Parkdrive: Yeah. And it took mine six hours to shut up.

Redhook: Holy—!

Parkdrive: Fortunately, I still had my gun and badge. I had the cuffs on him around midnight.

Redhook: Hey, you did the right thing, partner. I'm proud of you.

Parkdrive: Yeah. I did the right thing. Eventually.

    I felt, well, *strangely relieved* after dashing that off. And I think you can say I was filled with, well, what I think most people would call *resolve* to find Bruce and pry the innocent Lola from his clutches.
    Of course, when I got off the plane at Kahalui I hadn't the slightest idea where to look for the two of them. So while I was waiting by the luggage wheel I asked a fellow with a yellow lei and the unmistakable grin of an islander where, you know, he thought I might find a licentious man. He was very, um, *patient* as I put the word "licentious" into what I suppose you might call *practical* terms.

"Ah," he said, widening his eyes repeatedly at me like he was exercising his forehead. "You want Baby Makena beach." He leaned in closer and whispered. "They are naked there!"

Naked. That sounds like Bruce's modus—well, *way* of operating. Now to find Baby Makena...

IT'S ABOUT THE CLAMSHELL
by Barry Fest—*March 2*

    I must admit that Moliere, our email administrator, seems more than a little out of place on our staff of angular, bespectacled, and filmy-skinned morlocks.
    After assisting me with the glMail problem, Moliere began to take a peculiar interest in my own technical education. This is good, I submit. I believe in the virtues of all higher learning. Even mine. She is always bringing shiny new *objets* by my office, and while these amuse me, her interruptions take up, occupy, nay, *consume* parts of my working day that I do not, generally speaking, have to spare.
    The day after I mentioned to her the un-tattooed professionalism of my wife—Dr. Wharton-Stone—she brought me a little box with a green wire and antenna. "Hey boss," she said with her permanent grin and wide-eyed stare that looks right into the center of your pineal gland, "sweep your office with this baby. It finds little microphones, like the kind perfessional women like to plant in their husbands' offices."
    "Dr. Wharton-Stone," I said, "is a professional, not a 'perfessional.'"
    She giggled.
    A few days later she came by with a little gift, the kind of gift I hear young morlock women like to give to the older

men they admire. It was a watch with a binary readout. She wrapped the thick leather band about my wrist and started teaching me to read the little ones and zeroes before interrupting herself to finger the veins in my forearm.

When I told her I was a bit put off by her presumption, she giggled again and left. I still do not know how to turn off the alarm that beeps everyday at 00001101 o'clock.

And then there was the caffeinated chewing gum she gave me when I confided to her that my stamina, once the envy, model, nay, *idol* of the Belverton University Press editorial board, would no longer permit sustained, repetitive, physical activity. I chewed one stick of said gum and proceeded to compose, without so much as looking up at the sundial paperweight on the edge of my desk, an entire monograph on the Republican propensity to stutter.

Then yesterday I was seated behind my desk but facing away from it, so that I could work at the computer. Moliere came in, unannounced and uninvited, and approached me from behind.

Before I could turn to face her and say hello, she climbed up on the desk behind me and placed her feet on each of the two armrests of my chair. She pulled her dress back so that it would not cover my head, and put her knees forward of my ears. Had I turned my head left or right I would have struck a thigh with my nose.

I could not help but notice a green tattoo in the shape of a dagger on the inside of her right ankle. I also noticed a certain musky odor—an odor which I have never quite been able to place, but which I have always admired on women.

Before I could remark to her on the awkwardness of this position, she thrust into my hands a clamshell-shaped flipphone.

"It's the latest, boss," she said from somewhere over my head.

I flipped it open. "Goodness," I said. "It has a camera… and Internet access."

She reached around in front of me and flipped the phone closed. "That is *so* last year," she said. "I'm talking about the clamshell shape." She took my right hand in hers and rubbed my fingers along the shiny surface. "It's smooth. Don't you like it smooth?"

In fact, I did. There was something about the unadorned texture of the sleek metal clamshell that attracted, compelled, nay, *seduced* me.

"Does the perfessional let you touch her flip phone?"

"Of course."

"Is it smooth like mine?"

I do not like the use of possessives, and I had only just now noticed her presumptuous questioning of Dr. Wharton-Stone's cellular propensities. I rose abruptly.

"Moliere," I said, "I am afraid I am going to have to ask you to leave." I turned to face her. She was wearing a black T-shirt with white lettering that spelled out the words BOYS BLEED.

"I'll take that as a big hairy no," she said smiling. She covered her legs again with her longish skirt and stood off the desk. "Hey boss, you mind if I book a little early today? I wanna catch that show about Janet Jackson's nipples."

"Jan…nipples?"

"Yeah!" she squealed. "From the Super Bowl that time. They made a documentary of it on the pubic channel."

"I think you mean 'public' channel."

"What*ever*. Can I book?"

"Well. It *is* a documentary. On public television. Yes, by all means…*book*."

She departed the office, and I noticed again the peculiar *tingling*, as if an invisible extraterrestrial had fired a testosterone ray gun into my corduroys. I was momentarily overwhelmed by a chorus, concert, nay, *cacophony* of base urgings—thoughts which have as their invariable location a dark suburban basement lined with velvet and lit with red lights.

I sat down in my chair and looked to Dr. Wharton-Stone's business card, which I had taped to my monitor in case of emergencies just like this one. But the card had been defaced! The words "Professional Psychotherapist" captioning my wife's bold-fonted name had been changed, in pencil, to "Perfessional Psycho|the|rapist."

I hope you will not think me too paranoid when I say I suspect Moliere intends mischief for me.

WHERE DOES THE WORD "GIG" COME FROM?
by Desmond Cork—*March 9*

Hey cats. Well, the Babecat's still taking care of her grandmother in Maui. This grandmother I guess has a laptop or one of those email phones she lets the Babecat use because I've been getting emails from her. I guess the old babe is pretty sick because the emails are real short and they almost always end with the Babecat saying, "Gotta get going!" so I guess she's pretty busy.

But anyway I've got a lot of rock scholarship to do since people are writing me all the time and asking me things.

Here's a letter I got today from some cat named Adrian in Brooklyn.

> whoa des,
>
> OK, like ive been readin ur frickin ideas about rock n most of em r pretty on the nose.
>
> so ive got a question 4 u my man. remember b4 britney got married she got engaged. at least im pretty sure she did. I read it like on yahoo. heres what i wanna know. if musicians use the word gig

4 engagement does that mean they say gigged 4 engaged.

I mean did britneys bf say hey brit lets get gigged. did she call up ET n say here's the scoop im gigged. that night like did he get really frustrated w/havin her right there w/that nice round ass in those tight pants. n did he say cmon baby everybody does it once their gigged.

ya know. these things bug me. I think about them.

Yer boy,
Adrian

Okay good question, yeah? But he goes way wrong right off. See musicians don't say "gig" for "engagement." My boy Adrian has musicians confused up with comedians, and it's pretty well-known that comedians *hate* saying "engagement." When musicians say "gig" they say it out of memory of a cat who played guitar and whose name was Gig.

See, back in that time that people call the seventies? There was this punk rocker named Gregor Strayling who changed his name to Gig Spackle when he played one of the guitars in the punk band Caulk. One night Caulk was playing the Mudd Club in NYC. And that club is kind of small I guess and it got pretty packed? But NYC fire code cops knew it was okay because it was punk and punk doesn't care about rules, man. Still it got kind of tight what with about ninety kids covered in splinters of that gypsum board and doing the pogo in puddles of beer and whatnot.

Okay like you also should know that in those days? Department stores used to rent out empty racks to musicians real cheap so they could have a place to sleep without doing the hotel thing. So that night when Caulk was through playing their drums and guitars and stuff about fifty estro-crazed chicks screaming for friction followed them back to their racks at the Bowery Woolworth's.

The other members of Caulk were able to hide inside one of those lawn-weasel displays? But Gig was pinned to his rack by three of these chicks and the rest just lined up to take turns having their vicious estro way with him. The next morning they found him stretched out in a bin of flip-flops and he had nothing left to…contribute, yeah?

(I think he manages summer tours now. There are some pictures of him standing behind the B-52s looking real tired still.)

The night after that the cats at this other place called CBGB were real depressed, and Johnny Ramone said real famous-like, "Hey guys, let's get this one for the Gigger." And ever since then rockers have called rocking jobs "gigs."

Okay like I know what some of you cats are going to say. You're going to say, "Des. Dude. I just saw an old movie about Glen Miller and whatnot and they all said gig in it and that was like in the sixties and stuff."

Okay like I don't want to get all conspiracy on you? But those movies had the word "gig" put in *after* the thing those babes did to Gig on that night in the Bowery. See the woman is still on our backs cats and she doesn't want word about estro to leak out on the street. And that means the truth about Gig had to get buried with the truth about Oswald.

Think about *that* the next time some chick walks up to you all perky-like and says, "Like my rack?" She's talking about Gig, cats. And she's *rubbing it in*.

OUTSIDE THE BOX
by Barry Fest—*March 12*

Easter is not far off, and I am compelled to observe that the morlocks have a completely different view of the death of Jesus Christ than, say, the view of any person of genuine decency. (I am not saying that the morlocks are inferior humans. I submit, however, that until they are herded together into supervised camps, the superior humans will suffer considerable annoyance.)

Morlocks, in case you are so woefully out of step as to need the term explained, are the men (and the rare woman) who sate the soulless hunger of their Master, the machine. Morlocks, as I will demonstrate in a forthcoming monograph, are not merely servants of the technology but an actual part of it, only now and then pretending—in their tan Dockers and blue denims—to a creative humanity.

I was brought, dragged, nay, *hauled* to this conclusion just this afternoon, when Todd—our chief morlock at the Press—attempted to help me with a…no, let me start at the beginning. I received a glMail this afternoon from a person named Bev (heterosexual) who had just seen Mel Gibson's *The Passion of the Christ*. In her missive, she called me a spiritual descendant of said Christ's slayers.

I was distressed. Rarely have I been so misused, even by persons of wit. I was adrift in a reverie of self-pity when Todd walked past my open door. I called him into my office.

"Todd, what do you do when you receive a missive that lowers your self-approbation to its nadir?"

He walked around behind my desk and looked at the screen. "You're talking about an email, right?"

"Of course."

"You delete it here by pressing the 'delete' key," he said. And before I could shoo him off, his fat finger rammed that selfsame key, sending the missive from my accuser to the trash folder.

I felt a welcome and completely unexpected sense of relief.

"Now that I have you here, Todd, may I ask you a question?"

He looked at his watch. "Yeah, yeah, go," he said.

"What do you think of the crucifixion of Christ? Perhaps you know him as Jesus of Nazareth."

He warmed to the question instantly. "Interesting. Well, I think it shows that the Romans were able to think outside the box."

"I mean, what…metaphysical meaning do you draw from it?"

He paused for a moment, looking into the distance, then said: "Well, what I draw from it is that if you have a cross to send to an address, and a criminal to send to the same address, it's more efficient to make the criminal carry the cross than to ship them both separately."

Usually I would be jittery with impatience at this point. But the accusatory email made me want to prove to myself that I was, in fact, a kindly man, so I tried again. "What I mean, Todd, is what does the fact of Christ's crucifixion mean to you personally, if anything?"

"It demonstrates the importance of late binding," he said. "You know, a more primitive civilization would have put the cross together first, then nailed the criminal to it. But what the Romans did was they left the upright stakes in the ground permanently. Then whenever they needed to use them, they nailed the criminal to a fresh crosspiece and attached it to the stake with hooks. Very cool."

"But what…" I said, as the intemperate man inside me tried to assert himself, "what *supernatural* meaning do you take from it?"

Todd laughed. "There's nothing *supernatural* about it. It's good old-fashioned engineering."

And with that he left. When I'd had time to think about it, I dug my accuser's glMail out of the trash folder, clicked the reply button, and told her to go to hell.

MICKEY SNAKETAIL
by Nefertiti Snorkjutt—*March 13*

At last I have a chance to report on my search for the misogynist Bruce and the, well, *intrepid* Lola. Lola rescued me from Bruce's clutches, only to be taken by him to Maui, where I tracked them to a, um, *popular* nude beach called Baby Makena.

I decided to perform what I believe the police like to call a "stakeout." I thought that I had come rather well-prepared to look inconspicuous, but on the very first day a naked, well, *bitch* is I think the best word for her, a *bitch* with nipples stiff as a mannequin's walked past me and said, "Can you *sweat* through vinyl?" So I decided to sacrifice my last, well, what you might call *shred* of modesty and remove all of my clothes, save for the plastic strap holding the binoculars around my neck.

I used the binoculars to scan the beach dressed in that, um, nude, I suppose, *fashion* for days. Well, I took meals and slept, of course, but for the most part I was watching the beach. I sat on a white towel near a very wide parasol and pretended I was there to get a, yes, a *tan*.

The beach was covered with flesh, not all of it firm, and I could see naked conformists wading in the surf.

Through my binoculars I witnessed all sorts of misogynistic activity. "That's right," I muttered more than once, "all you want to do is help her get sunscreen on the parts she can't see. You sick bastard."

Then just a few days ago I was scanning the beach as usual when I saw one of the naked men looking through binoculars at *me*. He was a rather, well, *hirsute* individual seated with his legs crossed and with a laptop on the top of his, well, his *lap*. "Voyeur," I scoffed, then went on scanning the beach for signs of Bruce and the hapless Lola.

Then it happened again just a few, well, I think it was the very next day. Same man, only this time I noticed what looked like a rattlesnake's rattle tattooed on his arm. I thought little of it. I was convinced that Bruce and Lola were off avoiding the beach in daylight, so I would not be there for Mr. Snaketail to watch much longer. "Get a, well, *life*," I muttered.

I began to searching nearby beaches at dusk. One evening I found what looked to me like a deserted stretch of glassy sand beneath a row of small houses, each with a, um, oh, what is it called? Lanai? On a grassy ridge.

It was in this wet sand that I discovered an imprint of a pair of buttocks and just beneath this the imprint of two knees.

I had found the trail at last!

I was about to let out an uncharacteristic whoop of joy when I saw on the rocks separating the beach from the grassy ridge a figure typing into a laptop. It was Snaketail!

He didn't see me as I walked up, since his eyes were focused on the screen of his little computer. He was dressed now in shorts and a t-shirt. The t-shirt had the word MICKEY scrawled across the front in Disney lettering. The tip of the rattlesnake's rattle was just visible beneath his sleeve.

He looked up at me, I think shocked by my prox—well, by how *close* I was. He gave me a weird little grin with his mustached mouth.

"Are you writing in that thing about *me?*" I demanded.

He didn't answer but quickly slammed the laptop shut and ran off across the um, *tops*, I guess, of the rocks and down the beach. He had on these little sandals with jogger decals on the back. Odd, hm?

"Who is he?" I wondered. A Belverton University spy, sent to keep an eye on me? Was he the agent of some misogynist I once reformed, now with vengeance on his mind? Or had I stumbled onto a reality TV show—*Misogyny Island* or something?

But I was forgetting the buttocks, you know, the *imprints*. I ran back just as the low tide was filling them with surf, and snapped a photo with my little digital camera.

I looked to the lanais on the grassy ridge. A hard-target search was in order, I thought. But for that I would need some, well, *assistance*.

Surely I will find something akin to, well, *like* an anti-misogyny militia. They must have at least one of those in Hawaii, don't you think?

A ROUGH DRAFT
by Desmond Cork—*March 23*

Hey, cats. Well, I thought rock scholarship would help me keep my mind off the Babecat not being here but it looks like I need something else to go with it. And like when she left? I thought she was a little miffed at me for that night I spent at my best friend's half-sister Candy's house after I already told the Babecat I stopped being a babe-taste junky. And it kind of bothered me that she might be miffed so I sent her these emails that were like, "Babecat are you miffed?" and she sent emails back that were like, "No problem cat!" and "Say hi to Candy for me!" But still it's on my mind, cats.

So to take it off my mind I started writing a play about the ol' war in Iraq. Yeah. I'm calling it *You Cannot Polish A Kurd*. When it gets put on (and I'm like really hoping somebody puts it on) it'll pretty much end all the gun shooting over there. See basically the reason the gun shooting is still going on is that there's some things people haven't thought of yet and those things are in my play and when people see it they're going to go, "Whoa. I never thought of that before."

And then they'll change their minds.

Okay so like here's the story in summarization form which I pretty much got from thinking about peace and whatnot and then seeing this Jimmy Stewart movie last

Saturday. See the Americans rescue this Kurd from Saddam or Saddam's brother or nephew or some other evil cat related to Saddam or maybe friends with him and the next thing you know this Kurd gets elected to be the senator from Iraq and so he comes to Washington and they're so proud of him and all they make him Speaker of the House.

But before he comes to America? He's one of these cats who designs sets for musical comedies in Iraq and he's on the run from Saddam with all the other musical-comedy cats because Saddam hates music and hates to laugh. But the CIA? They track him down with those electronic birds that have phasers on stun and they convince him to be the guy who takes this farmhouse and uses his set-designing know-how to turn it into a bogus Al Qaeda training camp before the journalists show up and start taking pictures.

Yeah? He decides the right Feng Shui is to paint the torture room in these colors like paisley and this other color mauve (which I'm not real sure what those colors look like? But I hear those cats saying them all the time on *Queer Eye* or maybe it's that Martha show). Oh, and he also puts little lampshades on the hook parts of these meat hooks. How's this for some dialog:

> *CIA Dude*: Whoa like I don't know if I've ever seen a paisley pain palace previously. Maybe you and your assistant cats should look at these photos of a room just like it back in the ol' States.
>
> *Kurd*: Well like I'm not saying you're wrong or anything? But colors like that mauve color are right for the chi. I mean I can feel the chi. Can you feel the chi?
>
> *CIA Dude*: Dude. I'm from the US of A. I don't know chi from cheese.

Kurd: Then like don't take this the wrong way? But step off dude.

    I read this out of my notebook to this frosh babe I met on the quad and she was laughing so hard her face turned all red and she put her face between her legs which I think is tray hot when a chick does it. The only problem is I can see how it's all coming together and I'm thinking I'm going to need a real professional actor to play this Kurd. Maybe one of those *Saturday Night Live* cats or that Joe Pesci.

    But if like anyone out there is an actor or what have you? Hold off for now on the ol' pix and resumes. I still need to write a lot more and then talk somebody into putting it on.

JANET JACKSON'S EXAMPLE
by Barry Fest—*March 27*

I am certain I need not remind you of Ms. Janet Jackson's unconscionable behavior at the Super Bowl two or three years back.

Nevertheless, permit me to recapitulate. During the halftime of that estimable Bowl, Ms. Jackson "belted" out a high note, at which point her youthful male colleague tore off her blouse and bared her areola.

I thought little of this event when I heard its first report, but a recent documentary—*White Lust, Black Knobs*—aired on Belverton Public Television has resurrected the event as a topic of discussion in literate households, and has also, I am afraid, started an alarming trend among academic women.

At first I thought the phenomenon was limited to my classroom. Yesterday morning, Jessica Rynicker, a young lady with a 3.9 average, three acknowledged boyfriends, and a rumored lover on the faculty (one Sammy Stoles, who teaches the History of Ragtime elective)—a woman with fiery, blue, Andalusian eyes and whipped-caramel hair thick as Sophia Loren's—stood up to read aloud an excerpt from her postmodern analysis of that Penn & Teller program on Showtime. Libertarian magicians irk me as a class, and young Jessica's welcome review was scathing, vicious, ribald. At the very end of her reading, just as I was about to say, "Bravo," she threw up her hands and turned to the boy seated next to her. He dutifully stood, reached up (he was a bit short), and tore off her blouse. The class applauded and Jessica faced me, her nipples like a blank pink stare.

"Br—bravo," I said.

You may imagine my disquiet as I munched my lunchtime endive. Still, I had no reason to believe the fad had spread to anyone other than Ms. Rynicker and her hopping homunculus. Then, as I was leaving the cafeteria, a girl in a plaid skirt mounted a table, announced, "I'm doing my master's at Harvard!"—and tore off her white blouse with her own hands. Lacking a sense of drama, she tried to remove her bra by unhitching it in the back, and so lost the attention of her audience.

I was supposed to be home for dinner at precisely six that evening, but I was bewildered and spent a bit too much time with my therapist. When I walked in at six thirty, my wife—Dr. Wharton-Stone—was already seated at the dinner table with her parents, our guests. I attempted to apologize, but she launched into a scornful and haughty diatribe that ended with the words "and next time, you'll be locked out!" And on the word "out," her father, without looking away from his soup, reached over and ripped off her blouse.

I retired to my room without dinner.

A MESSAGE FOR DR. WHARTON-STONE
by Barry Fest—*March 31*

Good day, friends. My personal life has come to occupy an unfortunate, sad, nay, *grievous* position in the front of my consciousness. And, as you know, the front of one's consciousness is better left reserved for party politics.

After the blouse-tearing incident a few days ago, my wife—Dr. Wharton-Stone—came to me to apologize for her wanton imitation of a pop singer. An apology from Dr. Wharton-Stone is so unusual, and placed me in such a convivial mood, that I decided to tell her about Moliere, the email administrator at the Press. She rejoined my recollections with a chilly silence.

"She wants to have you in the naughty way, you idiot!" she raged moments later from her pillow in the dark. She snapped on the light and seized me by my pajama lapels.

"Sweetheart," I said, "there were no romantic lights, no dress with a split up the leg, not even a smidgen of lip gloss, no swooning. In fact, she was rather bossy."

Dr. Wharton-Stone stared at me for another moment, then took her pillow and went to sleep elsewhere.

The next day she appeared in my office—a rare treat for me, and thoroughly unexpected, as she had not visited the new offices since we moved here in 1999. "Beloved," I said from my desk as she walked in. "How did you find your way here?"

"Yahoo maps," she said. "Now where is this little *objet* of your libidinous *desir*? My God, is that her on her knees beneath your desk?!"

I rose abruptly and escorted her to the back of my desk, permitting her to see, with her own eyes, that beneath it was merely an empty space and hardly large enough to fit a tomcat, much less a full-grown woman. (Besides, stationing a woman beneath one's desk is strictly forbidden by Belverton University's Department of Ergonomics.)

Thus assured, she insisted that I take her out to find Moliere. After a few minutes navigating corridors, we found the young lady in question chatting with a colleague near a distant printer. She wore a black t-shirt with white lettering that spelled out the word HELLBOUND.

"Goth!" Dr. Wharton-Stone gasped. "A little Goth bitch!"

"Really, darling," I implored. "Not here, please!"

Dr. Wharton-Stone turned to me. She was pale and had a pained, hurt, nay, *injured* look upon her face. I do not believe I had ever seen it before. On second thought, I had seen it precisely once before: it was the look she had when her pet cat Shimmy took ill after she fed him a chicken leg.

That night I arrived home and gingerly entered the house, ready to be on my very best behavior. All was mysteriously quiet. I found Dr. Wharton-Stone in the upstairs den, in the dark. She was seated in an overstuffed chair in front of a window. As I came around in front of her I saw that she was completely unclothed.

"Don't close those drapes," she said. "I am getting a moon tan." On the table beside her lay a paperback novel. In the darkness I could make out only the words "Anne Rice" in a giant font that looked like it belonged on a sepulcher.

The next day she bought a full-length dress made of something that looked like black gossamer. *Tulle noir*, she called it when I inquired. The day after that she bought a variety of black t-shirts, each with one or more human skulls imprinted upon it.

On the fourth day she bounced—yes, Dr. Wharton-Stone *bounced*—over to me to show me the tattoo she had gotten on her shoulder. CARPE NOCTEM, it read, in large gothic letters. "And now," she said ebulliently, "I am going into the shower to shave off all of my pubic hair."

You may believe me when I tell you I was shaken. I drank, imbibed, nay, *quaffed* a flagon of red wine while Dr. Wharton-Stone stepped into the shower with a disposable razor and began defoliating a lifetime's growth of southerly forestation.

When she was finished, she was surprised to find, on one of her outer labia, a small, handwritten message.

"Barry!" she cried. I could tell from the tone of this cry that I had no time to dawdle. I walked briskly into the shower room and, closing my eyes (as is my wont), poked my head behind the plastic curtain.

"Open your eyes," she said. I did. She stood there, a sopping five-foot one-inch black-haired flower. "What does it say?" she asked, pointing. I squinted, but to no avail. I fetched a magnifying glass and knelt in the tub, unfortunately dampening the knees of my corduroys.

The message was in neat, cursive writing and a bluish ink. It said, simply, "Choose Jeffery."

On repeating this to my shivering wife, I could not keep indignation from coloring my tone. "Who," I demanded, "is Jeffery?"

"Oh my God…" she said. "On the night you proposed to me at the Met, Jeffery Mimms asked me to go with him to Coney Island." Her lower lip, purpling slightly in the cold, began to quiver. "I was supposed to get that message fifteen years ago!"

She reached a hand up, grasped the side of her face, and began to sob. "Nyagh!" she shrieked. "Nyaghhhh!!!!!"

Later, in bed, she lay on her side facing away from me and sobbing. I touched her, and she pulled away as if attempting to break my fingers. "It is not necessarily a bad thing," I suggested in a whisper. "Fate may not be telling you that you belong with Jeffery Mimms. It may simply be telling you that you should have been shaving since graduate school."

The sobbing stopped. "This house," she said nasally, "is not big enough."

So I left my home to spend the night on the sofa in my office at the Press. As I nodded off, my eyes fell upon a mugshot of myself from my stalking days. It had been framed years before by a colleague of comical proclivity, and still hung on my wall to remind me that I, too, had misspent moments in my youth.

"My youth…" I muttered as I fell asleep, and wondered…whatever happened to Jeffery Mimms?

STALKING MONDI
by Barry Fest—*April 3*

Friends, I come to you contrite and indignant at once. What fuels my contrignation (as it shall be called henceforth) is my reflection on the framed mugshot of a younger version of myself hanging on the wall of my office at the Press. This embarrassing photograph, snapped in a glaring white light, forced me to recall a time when my head was forcibly checked for lice by a supple policewoman wearing red lip gloss and using any excuse to rub her stiffening nipples against my youthful pectoralis. The contrite part of the contrignation will become apparent from the sordid and sorry story that follows, a sequence of events that brought me to the point of opening wide and saying "ah" for that same burly policewoman so that she could check my cheeks for secreted cyanide.

How, you surely must wonder, could I, a cited scholar, come to such a pass? It was as simple as it was strange. I was just out of college, sitting on the marble steps of the bursar's building, sucking an orange popsicle and reading, on the back of a record album, the biography of Mondi McDade, lead singer for the pop-rock group Blynx. It said, "Mondi is the more reclusive of the group. Says Mondi: 'Sometimes I wish I just had someone who gets *me*.'"

Well, *I* "got" her, and she did not even know my name! Soon I found myself in her constant company (imagined, of course), enlightening her with my unique perspective on current events, my surprising hipness, and the thoughts that would later become the contents of my monograph, *Why Not a Square? Alternative Dating Strategies for Women in the Recording Industry*. I talked to her in my apartment, walking down the street, in the waiting room of the chiropractor's office. Growing tired of the charade, and knowing I had so much to offer a real power-popper if only she could recognize me if she passed me on the street, I discovered her address and mailed her six long-stemmed roses, a picture of myself reading Plath, and the aforementioned monograph, signed. It worked, in a way. The burly policewoman was at my house less than three days later. She did not take me into custody on that visit. She had, she said, some "questions to ask."—And she asked them whilst swaggering bustily, winking, and licking her lips. Somehow, I believed, this femcop had learned how things were between Mondi and me and wanted me all to herself.

That was when I deserted my home and hied myself to the graveled lot behind Mondi's house. I dug a deep hole there after midnight one night, and before sunrise I climbed in, placing over the entryway a flowerpot containing one erect, long-stemmed rose.

It was a crafty plan. I laughed at the ingeniousness of it all, there in the dark of the vertical tunnel. Now no one could deprive Mondi of me! And it was only a matter of time before she got curious about the long-stemmed rose in the flower pot, walked over, and...

As I was thinking about it, I began to choke. I was a lover, after all, not an engineer, and had forgotten to provide myself with an air supply. The next thing I knew I was on a stretcher trying to talk through an oxygen mask. "I am Barry Fest, the love-tutor of Mondi McDade," I said to the nearest paramedic. "I am willing to negotiate!"

So I was checked for lice and interrogated by men and women who did not understand the first thing about love between a man and a woman. And so I say to you, if you are ever in a Belverton police station and you happen upon my photograph in their big book, please have some compassion. If loving too much is a crime, I confess.

SHOULD ROCK BANDS EVOLVE?
by Desmond Cork—*April 14*

Hey cats. I'm pretty stoked about this play I'm writing called *You Cannot Polish A Kurd*. And like, now? Well the other day these drama cats said they wouldn't put it on for real but that they would like read it out loud in front of people and so they're going to do that in a few weeks from now at Chomsky Hall on campus.

So I guess until then I can still do rock scholarship. I got this one question today and I think it should stop a lot of rumors about rock bands, yeah?

> Des Love,
>
> My name is Riot, and I'm the music critic for *Please Thrill Me* magazine.
>
> We're having a little dispute here among the editors. Two schools of thought, hm? One says that rock bands should always evolve. The other one says that rock bands should find the one thing they do best and just keep doing it.

We can't wait to hear what you have to say.

You suck hard,
Riot

Whoa. I suck hard. From a punk babe especially one named Riot that is a really big compliment cats.

But this Riot babe kind of makes a mistake. See it isn't all one way or the highway. Sometimes you don't want rock bands to evolve but other times they evolve and it's cool.

Like back in the early nineties there was this band? They called themselves Milwauky and they liked to play rhythm and the blues but with less of an emphasis on rhythm and substituting the blues with a bicycle horn.

So Milwauky was doing this tour of Japan and right on the stage one night they just evolved. It was gruesome cats. They were finally killed by the Japanese army after eating half the city of Fukuoko.

But when most bands evolve people are cool with it. Especially when they evolve into Seven-Eleven managers or rollerblade salesmen. There was this band called Cha-Cha Spittoon? Four of them evolved into building superintendents and the drummer won a rubber band-playing contest on Leno.

But the sad factoid is that a lot of rock stars are too busy hiding from chicks to evolve. You know how if you go backstage at a concert you see clumps of babes with t-shirts that say things like WILL DO BOBBY FOR FOOD. They're all freaked out on estro and stealing the rock stars' powers to evolve by siphoning the powers off like gas out of their dads' BMWs.

It kind of bums me when I think of all the rock stars that might have evolved if they hadn't been jumped by babes over and over. But like the Japanese are probably better off.

THE ALTRUISTIC STALKER
by Barry Fest—*May 2*

Yesterday was a day filled with prejudice against my humanity, my friends. It was a day of near, approximate, nay, *virtual* evil.

You know already the sad adventure that was my pursuit of the lovely Mondi McDade, back in the late 1980s—a pursuit that ended in considerable embarrassment and inconvenience for me. Nevertheless, I continue to sense an affinity for Mondi, the lead singer for the defunct rock band Blynx; an affinity that my psychiatrist wife—Dr. Wharton-Stone—finds personally repelling but professionally fascinating.

The aforesaid virtual evil came this morning in the form of a certified missive delivered to my office by the United States Postal Service. Here it is in its entirety, *sans* intimidating letterhead:

Dear Mr. Fest:

Pursuant to my discussions with my client, Mondi McDade, you are to cease sending to her home, to her place of business, and to the homes and businesses of her representatives, relatives, and friends, any and all unrequested items, including, but not limited to, notes, letters, monographs, memorabilia, flowers, Mensa credentials, necklaces, jams, jellies, office supplies, hip-hugging jeans, quinine, figs, paper hats, candles, rubber heels, zoo souvenirs, incense, wicker accessories, leg-warmers, and taffy. You are to cease sending balladeers to sing and actors to recite. You are neither to approach her nor to send her email, specifically, you are not to send her email that begs, cajoles, or attempts to initiate what a reasonable person would construe as "banter."

In brief, Mr. Fest, you are to forget that Ms. McDade exists until such unlikely time as she finds the need to invite you, in writing, to remember her. If she ever tours again and you find yourself in the audience, you must sit at least thirty rows back (in a large venue) or ten rows back (in a small venue). If she chooses to perform in a small club, you must listen from the street.

Ms. McDade has conveyed to me that she is usually very grateful for her fans and their continued support, but that you have clearly crossed the line that separates fan from crazy oddball. After reviewing a sample of the materials you have sent to her over the years, I can only say that she is being too kind.

It is my duty to remind you that stalking is a crime in both your state and Ms. McDade's. Should you continue your harassing attentions, we will have no recourse but to turn the matter over to the authorities.

    Sincerely,
    Rutger Flint, Esq.
    Flint, Snocter & Rimbeaux

I find the entire tone of this letter disheartening. And I really must object to the characterization of my attentions as "stalking" and "harassment." Had you read the back of the same album cover that I had read, and had come to the same conclusion I had come to—that a woman you never met was in desperate need of your talents, your personality, and your every thought on every subject—you would know precisely what I mean. I am not some bumpkin who wants to take a Country & Western singer back to his cabin to bake his bucolic pies, raise his rural kiddies, and help him fasten the snaps on the seat of his faded denims. No, I want to give her what she needs. I am utterly selfless in the matter. Surely there must be an exemption in the stalking laws for those who pursue in the spirit of intellectual charity, mustn't there? If not, shouldn't there be? Would you accuse Jesus of Nazareth of "stalking" humanity with the Sermon on the Mount? Or Moses of "stalking" the Hebrews with the Ten Commandments?

I believe my point is more than made. And, if you go back and reread the letter, you will see that even her lawyer admits she may one day invite me, in writing, to commune with her again. Were it not for encouragements like these, the insinuations of third parties on the consequences of passion would be too much for me to bear.

A MORAL FOR THE KURD
by Desmond Cork—*May 12*

Hey cats. Last night a whole bunch of people went over to Chomsky Hall on campus to see these actor cats read my play called *You Cannot Polish a Kurd* out loud. And like, a lot of them? A lot of them were pals of the Babecat and me who wanted to see what was up with the ol' play I've been talking about for months so I guess you could say they were like curious. But then these other cats were there who I don't know and like I wasn't sure why they were there unless they were on dates and stuff and wanted to be entertained and that made me kind of nervous. Because like when you take a chick out to be entertained? Sometimes it's fun to mock out the ol' entertainer. I know because I do that sometimes and it's a blast.

But my best friend's half-sister Candy who I was with (the Babecat's out of town, cats) said the audience was down with the whole tone or something and I heard them laughing all right but like if there are any other playwriting cats out there is it just me or does it always seem like the audience is laughing in the wrong place?

I told this to Candy and she said: "De-es! Hon-ey! They're supposed to laugh!"

(Then she put her hand on my leg way up high, almost to the ol' girlfriend zone.)

Even though Candy said it was supposed to go funny? Still there was this one major non-funny part. Okay, first Saddam is executed. I guess that's kind of funny. But then the Kurd—who's the senator from Iraq and Speaker of the House—is run over by a car with red state plates and then he dies and then he tries to get into heaven. Just as he's getting past the cloudy part to the gates and whatnot he sees this cat in white come out to meet him and it's Saddam.

Saddam: Whoa, Kurdsy, where you going?

Kurd: Heaven, dude! I can see it right over there!

Saddam: No can do, Kurds. You're not on the list.

Kurd: Whoa. You're saying you got into heaven and I didn't? How does that work, dude? You were like this brutal dictator who offed a million cats. I ended up Speaker of the House in the US of A. This is way harsh.

Saddam: You were kind of stuck up, though, dude. It's all about not being stuck up. Where does it say like in any good book, "Thou shalt not be a brutal dictator"? But pride goeth before a fall and whatnot—that's in every good book ever written. It's in magazines even. And what it means in modern words is hey don't be stuck up.

Kurd: You're saying you weren't stuck up? Like what about all those pictures of your head that you put outside on big banners and stuff? And like every place there was a stop sign right next to it was this tray huge statue of the Sad.

Saddam: Self-help, dude. I had a butt-load of need-a-hug issues. You should have gotten that. So let me ask you: You have need-a-hug issues?

Kurd: No.

Saddam: Easy in your own skin? Yeah?

Kurd: I guess.

Saddam: They *made* hell for cats like you, dude.

A guy is going to hell and he learns a moral and a lesson…Maybe I'm old school but I just don't see what's so funny about that.

BRUCE AND THE PATRIOT ACT
by Nefertiti Snorkjutt—*May 19*

Well, I have been *quite* busy since my last entry. It has been a very long time, and has been, um, oh, *arduous*, I suppose is the right word, but I have, um, *tracked them down at last*, you know? Bruce and Lola, I mean. And I am at this moment surrounded by local militiamen, some of whom are quite, well, some of whom are misogynists I would love to take a week to reform. Each. In a soundproofed cellar.

Noth—well, *few* things make me run warmer than the thought of a man in uniform. Especially one whimpering, "Please stop."

When I wrote to you last, I had just followed the trail of Bruce and the valiant Lola to a ridge of middle-class lanais above a beach in Maui. But there the trail went dead.

(I suppose I should explain that a "lanai" is a, well, a *veranda* of sorts, but with a roof over it. And all of the lanais on the ridge above the beach had, well, *movable* walls, presumably so that the men and women inside could cavort unseen.)

I couldn't very well do a hard-target search of these lanais myself. I would have loved to, let me tell you, but I was informed by the first young lady I attempted to deputize that the people in those lanais are protected by the police, and that these police are, well, under the *impression* that men and women have the so-called "right" to do whatever they want to one another as long as their walls are up and nobody complains later.

I returned to Belverton for a while to save money (the hotels here are, well, it *is* Hawaii, so they are rather, um, *dear*). But when I got back to Maui a week ago I had no more, well, no *fresh* ideas about where to search. I went out to the ridge of middle-class lanais and began to brood. I sat down on the grass in front of the lanai nearest the beach. I was dressed inconspicuously in thick-soled flip-flops and jeans. My blouse was porous enough to admit the evening breeze, so my, well, *nipples* had begun to *peak*.

As they did, three young men and two ladies walked past on the beach, lit only by the moon and some wash from the lanais behind me. The extra man sauntered over to me and said, "You make me ache, baby."

"Push off, thong-boy," I said, "or I'll make you ache where you didn't even know you had, well, *things that can ache*."

His t-shirt flapped as he ran to catch up with his friends. "The police state," I thought, "should do its job and crack down on these moonlight marauders."

If I, well, if I were a *cartoon* a little light bulb would have switched on above my head at that moment. I took out my cell phone and dialed up the local police. I reported that a dark-complexioned man named Bruce with a large, cylindrical object in his jeans had kidnapped a young woman and had brought her to Maui to, well, *terrorize someone*, and this *someone* was most likely a mainstream American. You know, a white male heterosexual enslaved to the female orgasm. Middle-aged. Fat. Wearing a suit.

"I'm putting you through to the FBI, ma'am," said the desk sergeant, interrupting my description. When the FBI got on the line I repeated the story.

"We'll be inside those lanais in no time," said the baritone agent.

"You're not worried about the rights of the so-called innocent?" I asked.

He laughed. "This," he said, "is a job for the US Patriot Act if I ever heard one. Haven't those bastards on Lanai Ridge heard of the greater good? You unclench and I'll have the PANDAS out there in half an hour."

Forty-five minutes later, Julian—the baritone agent—and the PANDAS (Patriot Act National Defense Attack Squad) had the entire ridge surrounded.

(I know that—or at least I *suspect* that—my colleagues will, well, *object* to my using the Patriot Act for any reason. But I say: if it's there, why not use it to shackle a few misogynists to the wall of my cellar, hm?)

I have to say that Julian and the PANDAS caused quite a bit of mayhem that night. I remember dogs screaming and women barking. A man in old-fashioned pajamas and a lick of white hair that stood straight up refused to let the boys into his house at first. After the PANDAS wrestled him to the ground, they searched his house while I, well, *kicked* him repeatedly and tried to console his wife (a woman with superb gluteus muscles for her age but with a face that would boil raindrops).

"We're looking for a man who can speak directly to a woman's biology!" I explained. She didn't seem to understand. "It's a diabolical skill!" I went on. "He must be prevent—well, *stopped.*"

But there was no Bruce in that lanai.

Finally, at the center of the perimeter, the last lanai was encircled. The PANDAS crept closer, their snub-noses unholstered. One of them produced a bullhorn and handed it to Julian.

"Come out with your pants up!" Julian urged those inside. There was no response. Then Julian—a man with a bottom so vast that it reached all the way to his neck, giving him the appearance of a large hamster with a sweaty face—approached the front door.

Just as he was taking the safety off his pistol, the door opened and Lola appeared. "Bruce?" she repeated, when she learned why we were there. "Bruce went back to Belverton yesterday."

At that moment, one of the nearby PANDAS cried: "Somebody's in there!"

"Charge!" shouted Julian. Ten PANDAS crashed through the door, knocking Lola to the ground. I helped her up and slapped her face.

"Hussy!" I cried. (I still don't—well, I *still* don't know where *that* came from.)

I followed the PANDAS into the lanai, and there, in the corner, was...Mickey Snaketail!

He was seated at a laptop and grinning at us from under his little mustache. His snaketail tattoo was just visible under his shirtsleeve. As the men approached him, he deserted the laptop, opened the movable wall of the lanai, and escaped into the darkness. The PANDAS outside let him pass, mistaking the snaketail tattoo for Justice Department insignia.

So tomorrow I will be on my way back to Belverton—and when I get there, Bruce will have a piece of my, well, *mind.*

TONGUE EXERCISES
by Barry Fest—*May 26*

I have been riding a strange rollercoaster, my friends. My late adventures command my attention in ways so primal that even I, the executive editor at a bleeding-edge university press, can barely comprehend them.

I am still living in my offices at the Press, having been exiled there by my wife—Dr. Wharton-Stone—after she found a disturbing message tattooed on one of her freshly-shaven labia. During this exile my office has become my habitat. For the past two months, Dr. Wharton-Stone has refused to admit me to our domicile because—and I do not fault her for this—there is something about my face, my demeanor, my chewing and scratching that she cannot bear while the message on her labia is still visible. So I am waiting, pining, nay, *longing* for the day when her pubic pelt has grown back sufficiently to cover that missive from hell.

And headaches plague me, my friends. Headaches that chant: "Three ventis a day…three ventis a day…why not four…why not four…"

So last night I lay there in the dark, as usual, in my white shirt, black pants, and beige blanket. I managed to nod off at last, to be awakened three short hours later by Moliere, our individualistic glMail administrator. She stomped into the office dressed in a black tank top, a long dress, and thick, black, masculine boots.

Owing to the paucity of fabric in her shirt, more of the dragon tattoo was visible than usual: the snarling head licking her nape, the wings sleeving her arms, the tail reaching down for something below her waist.

She took a long breath of the office air. "Mmm," she said. "I love the smell of nerd in the morning. It smells like… pencil rubber."

Then she winked at me and walked out.

Later, I received a glMail from an old flame (bisexual) who had recently enlisted her lithe form and moist lips in a campaign to seduce each Democratic presidential candidate out of the mainstream, but I could see only the subject line. The body of the message was mysteriously blank.

I summoned Moliere and sat back in my seat, my temples throbbing. When I had finished describing the problem to her, she stood next to me and bent over to tap my keyboard. Her dress was quite close to my face, and I could see the little fabric ribs in her tank top bracing the firm circularities that were her breasts. Circularities from which, owing to my headache, I failed to avert my eyes.

"Like 'em?" she asked.

Friends, I tell you without reservation that I did, in fact, like them. What I did *not* like was that she was watching me watch her without telling me. "Please, Moliere," I said, and cleared my throat.

"Sorry," she said and turned back to the keyboard. She tried to rest one hand on the computer table, but looked away too soon and missed the top. Her hand ended up on my thigh.

She snapped it back. "*Whoops*," she said. "Bit of a fox pass, eh, boss?"

The headache I was enduring provoked me to winces.

"Problem, chief?" she asked.

"Headache."

"Really? Well, I know how you can fix that up!"

She sat on the desk beside me, positioning herself so that my face was virtually lying in her lap.

"Could you have a seat in front of the desk?" I asked. She rolled her eyes and plopped down in a gray, felt-upholstered chair.

"Cool," she said. "Now, you need to understand what causes most headaches in men."

"And what is that?"

"Weak tongue."

"Tongue?"

"Yup!"

"Forgive my skepticism, Moliere, but…*tongue?*"

"Well, let's do a little test!" she said. She balled her hand into a fist and thrust it in front of my face sideways. "Try pryin' it open."

"You must be joking."

"Come on, boss! I won't make it too tight, if that's what you're scared of."

After several similar exhortations, I finally acquiesced, placing my tongue tentatively against her salty flesh.

"C'mon!" she whined, grinning. "Press it! Split it open for me!"

And press I did. But try as it might, my tongue was unable—desperately unable—to pry apart her fingers.

"All right," I said finally. "That's enough. I concede I am cursed with a febrile glossus."

My tongue ached a bodybuilder's ache.

She sat back in her chair. "Whatever. Most men don't know how important it is to have a good strong tongue. Then they get in a situation."

"A situation?"

"Yeah. A situation where their tongues need to act out. But if they've got flabby ones? They end up back in their own racks with these splitting headaches!"

"Yes…yes, I see. A situation, for example, where a man has to give a speech before the UN General Assembly?"

"Um, yeah," she said, rolling her eyes slightly. "Like if a man has to give a speech before the UN General Assembly."

(I noted, for a future journal entry, that Moliere pronounced all three syllables of the word "general" with equal emphasis, as a recent immigrant or an elocution teacher might do.)

She paused for a moment, then said: "Tell ya what, boss. If you want, I can get you something to help out with tongue exercises."

"Well…can you get it now?"

"Sure! Hold on. I got a few back in my cube."

She returned from said cube a few moments later. In her hands she carried a shiny red ball with black straps attached.

"You put this ball in your mouth," she said. "Then you tighten these straps around the side of your head. But not too tight or you'll get a mouth-ache. Now, once you've got it in place, press against the ball with your tongue. It's isometric."

"Hmm," I said. "Isometric."

It sounded promising.

"Sure. Start with three sets of twenty reps a day, and work your way up to five sets of fifty reps."

"I suppose I owe you something for this contraption," I said. "It can't be free."

"Oh, it isn't."

She gave me a curious little smile as her eyes looked through my eyeballs and into the back of my skull.

"There's nothing *free* about it," she said.

Then she turned and left, without naming the price.

I stared at the empty space where she had been standing, and marveled. Over the past several days, I had mentioned my headaches to at least a dozen colleagues, and none could do more than offer me an aspirin from a tin. Yet this young lady was helping me to understand and correct the problem at its source.

I am sorry to have to admit it, but it appears that I may have underestimated our Moliere.

STANDARDS
by Desmond Cork—*May 27*

Babecat's back! She was in Maui for the last three months or so, which I think is an Indian reservation someplace. It was a family emergency and whatnot. That's my Babecat, yeah? Who else is going to fly out to the middle of noplace just so she can hold her grandma's hair while the old bag ralphs?

Anyway she comes back with this darker skin that they get down south and stuff and with this big smile on her face from doing good. And what am I in the middle of? Polishing up the ol' play, cats. It's tray happening. I can't even break away to show the Babecat how much I yearn (especially now that she has the darker skin).

So anyway I've been sending out my play (it's called *You Cannot Polish a Kurd*) to people who put on plays for real and don't just read them out loud like they did at Chomsky Hall that time and now the Belverton Board Treaders on Veblen Street in the Futon District say they want it to be their summer play and I even get to direct.

I told them that I have like really high standards? They said that was okay but then later they called back and asked me to give an example of the standards. That made me say "um" a lot cats because it's been a real long time since I thought about my standards except to know that they're like, high. So after I stopped saying "um" I made up some stuff they didn't buy so I told them I'd call them back after I thought about it and maybe doodled down some notes.

The doodling helped me think and whatnot? So I called them up and told them that my standards mean like I have to have the right dudes and babes in all the parts and that doesn't just mean they can act it out. It means they've got to get it. They've got to get *me*, yeah?

The Board Treaders' dude-in-charge? His name is Phil. Phil asked me how I thought I would test to see if people got me. You know, like at tryouts. That was like a really good question cats because I'd never thought of that before. So I told him I'd call him back and I sat down to have a good think. And yeah I doodled and it helped.

Here's what I came up with. If you're a dude, you have to stand and face me and put your right hand on my left shoulder while I put *my* right hand on *your* left shoulder. Then you stare into my eyes while I stare back into your eyes. If you can do that without making me giggle then my standards say you're good to go.

If you're a babe we have to hug and see how long it can remain what they call professional. For you non-director cats it's really easy to tell when a hug stops being the professional kind. I don't want to get technical? So let's just say it has to do with *grinding*.

I would have the no-grind rule for all chicks trying out except maybe the ones trying out for the part of Hotsie. 'Cause Hotsie is a grinder, cats.

HOTSIE
by Desmond Cork—*June 3*

Okay, now that I'm a director of a play and all and I'm looking for hot babes to cast I have to explain to the Babecat that when chicks at the tryouts grind up against my zipper it's really no fun for me at all. It's like a professional evil? But a professional evil that's really necessary if what you're looking for is a hot babe to play a hot-babe part.

Here's what I mean. The Belverton Board Treaders on Veblen Street in the Futon District are putting on my play *You Cannot Polish a Kurd* and I'm on the hunt for some hot babes to play the hot-babe parts. And the hottest babe that I wrote in my whole play is this babe named Hotsie, and a lot of chicks sent in their resumes but this one hot chick who now gets to be Hotsie so I guess that makes her the winner? She read the script and she thought it would be real cool if Hotsie was on stage more and had more words to say. At first I thought, "Whoa. Step off babe." But right then she yawned and arched her back so I didn't say that at all, cats. Like I don't remember what I really said? But whatever it was when I said it, it made her have this big smile.

So I wrote this whole extra part near the middle where Hotsie meets the Kurd after he gets elected senator from Iraq and the other senators make him Speaker of the House but before he gets run over by the bus with the red state plates. I wrote it after the hot babe said we should improv, which she said means she gets to make up her own lines and really professional writers just put down what she says only with punctuation that never gets said out loud anyway. Oh and in this improv? I pretended to be the Kurd. This is what me and the hot babe said to each other and I wrote it down and made it the new part of my play:

> *Hotsie*: Mr. Speaker? Like I think I can see your thong showing over the top of your pants.
>
> *Kurd*: Whoa. That's like not cool? I thought I could wear thongs any way I wanted in the US of A.
>
> *Hotsie*: Dude, it's way not cool. Show me a place in the Constitution where it says you can wear a thong over the top of your pants.
>
> *Kurd*: Okay but like you have to show me where it says in the Constitution that you can ask me about my thong nasty.
>
> *Hotsie*: Okay like it says you have freedom of speech in the Constitution? But where does it say you have the freedom to use the word "nasty" when you can't think of the right noun? Show me that.
>
> *Kurd*: I'll show you that as soon as you show me where it says you have the right to ask me to show you where it says something in the Constitution.
>
> *Hotsie*: It says you have freedom of association in the Constitution but it doesn't say you have the freedom to associate with that hag you live with off-campus.

I know, dudes. How she gets to freedom to be in an association in the last part is something I haven't figured out yet. It's just that when we improvved it? It sounded right somehow.

I let the Babecat read it and she got pretty mad cats because she figured that the hag in that last part is her. And I'm like, "Whoa. Babecat. Hey. It's like you know how comedians are always like, 'Hey my wife, she gives bad head'? Well the wives are okay with it because they know it's the ol' comedian's job, yeah? So like where Hotsie says the Kurd lives with a hag? Hey I mean, ya know?"

And she went into the bedroom and locked the door, cats. I counted up to 1700-banana and then went to sleep on the ol' sofa.

THE GOERING CAMPAIGN
by Nefertiti Snorkjutt—*June 10*

Well, you can have your Clintons and your Obamas and, oh, the other ones are, oh, McCains and I suppose Giulianis, too. I am afraid I must find a third-party candidate. Recently I was informed of the, well, *insurgency* of Congressman Slappy Goering—a former comedian who is also deep.

(Goering's running mate is Stiv Corkman, the actor who played the pig's head in the 1990 remake of *Lord of the Flies*.)

Goering is running on the Reformed Misogyny ticket, and is the only candidate in the race who has pledged not to have an erection before Election Day.

I first heard of Goering's promise when I got back from Maui, where I was attempting to, well, *rescue* a slut named Lola from the depredations of the man known only as "Bruce." I had decided—well, *determined* that I would pay Bruce a little visit and get some satisfaction for his having wasted three months of my life, hm?

So last week I knocked at his door. There was a long pause; then the door opened a crack exposing the right side of his face.

"Professor Snorkjutt, ma'am?" he asked.

I shouldered in and cuffed him around. When I paused to catch my breath he apologized profusely—well, perhaps not profusely, but at least *abundantly*—for having stolen off with Lola, then confessed to me that he felt so guilty for misbehaving that he had signed on to work in the campaign of the aforesaid Slappy Goering.

"You'd like him," he said with a flinch. "He's a former comedian who is also deep."

When he described the campaign, I could not help suspecting that Bruce was, in fact, engaged in some misogynistic ruse. And the more I pond—well, *thought* about it, the more I came to suspect that the entire Goering Campaign might be some beard for misogynists who want to look romantic to the innocent women they are bamboozling.

As destiny, well, perhaps not destiny but at least *fate* would have it, Goering was an avid reader of the adventures in Maui that I posted on the Internet, so for him I am a minor celebrity. I sent him the following email in a blatant—or at least *obvious*—attempt to cash in on my fame:

> Dear Congressman Goering,
>
> I would love to lend the, um, *credibility* of the Snorkjutt mystique to your campaign, but this will require an interview. That is, an interview of you conducted by me.
>
> Yours very truly,
> Nefertiti Snorkjutt

He sent me one back.

> Snorky Snorkworth Snorkington,
>
> Loved your wacky adventures in Maui! Hey Snorkster…we gots Brucey! Right here on our shoo, if you know what I mean (nyuk, nyuk, nyuk)!

Oh, and pursuant (nyuk!) to your request for a tête-à-tête (nyuk! nyuk!) I can only say, bring it on! Wifey-poo will be there. The two of you can chat down mansters!

Counting the Seconds,
Slappy Slappingham Slapperino

It took me a half day to realize that "mansters" meant "men."—And wifey-poo? Why, if I were his wife I would, well, *bitch* slap him.

OPENING NIGHT
by Desmond Cork—*July 5*

Big night for me last night cats. It was opening night for my play *You Cannot Polish a Kurd*, which is being put on by this group on Veblen Street called the Board Treaders.

I think it went okay. Those articles in the paper that these cats write who review plays and whatnot? They don't come out until Friday this being Belverton and whatnot but people seemed to be laughing a *lot*.

I don't like to brag? But I counted over a hundred laughs and that's pretty good. And when I was writing it? I didn't even know it was a comedy.

I had kind of a buzzkill about a week ago though. The dude-in-chief of the Board Treaders—Phil—was real particular that I change some of the words to talk about those family values you probably heard of. He got pretty excited too and said some stuff I didn't get about Huns and vandals and Rome, which I guess used to be a much bigger city than it is now. I kind of called Phil some bad names and then when I ran out of names I made these hoots like an owl while he was talking which was kind of funny if you saw his face trying to stay all calm. But his wife kept being sarcastic to me so I gave in and she stopped.

So I added this speech at the very end for Hotsie who falls in love with the Kurd and then he's hit by this bus with red state plates and now she misses him. She's in the cemetery looking at his gravestone with Shlesh, the Kurd's teenage son that he got from this chick he was married to before he met Hotsie back when he was still in Iraq designing those backgroundy things for musical comedies. (I added Shlesh so the Kurd could have a family, which I guess is really important for family values.)

Here's the part I added in. I guess it's going to help keep the ol' Huns from wrecking America the way they wrecked Rome:

> *Hotsie*: Whoa. Kurdsy.
>
> *Shlesh*: Hi Pop!
>
> *Hotsie*: Well, it's graduation day for Shlesh. I guess he'll be going off to college. It's like tragic and sad and all that you got hit by that bus with red state plates and couldn't be here but hey, look both ways, yeah?
>
> *Shlesh*: I love you Mommy.
>
> *Hotsie*: And Mommy loves Shleshy but right now Mommy's talking to Daddy, yeah?
>
> *Shlesh*: Aww…
>
> *Hotsie*: Whoa. Shleshmeister. Don't go watery on me. We're a family and families have like values.
>
> *Shlesh*: Aww…

Hotsie: Here. Put your mouth on this.

Shlesh: Oh cool.

Hotsie: Well Kurdsy I guess I should say that the house? It's way empty without you in it. Not so hard you have to work up to it. Like I go in the kitchen—little circles, flicker, flicker, little flickers—and I think about how I used to be married to the very first Kurd to become Speaker of the House. Oh yeah, rhythm. I like get letters? Yeah, I get letters from girls just starting out who want to know how they can meet a Kurd who might become Speaker of the House and I—okay okay back off. Um, put your mouth on one of these.

So I guess I kind of sold out a little, cats. I mean family values wasn't my idea, but hey I guess if you're graduating from high school and you get adopted by a really hot babe? There's nothing wrong with being close and all especially if it's going to help protect this bounteous land of ours.

RAVES FOR THE KURD
by Desmond Cork—*July 10*

Okay cats, not like I want to brag or anything? But these articles that the reviewers wrote about *You Cannot Polish a Kurd* came out yesterday and like most of them were written by really smart review-writing cats. Like me I'm still pretty surprised by how smart they are.

Here's my favorite one so far. It's from the *Belverton Bugle* which is this newspaper that real people read with pictures of people who won kabillions and TV stars on the front if they just got arrested or one of their nipples showed and somebody caught it:

> Last Friday saw the opening of Desmond Cork's *You Cannot Polish a Kurd* at the Board Treaders Theatre on Veblen Street. What you learn quickly when you enter the theatre is that story, characterization, and style have all been discarded by Mr. Cork in a bravura *tour de force* of postmodern insight.
>
> Ostensibly about an Iraqi Kurd who is first hired by the CIA to decorate the "Al Qaeda camps" in northern Iraq, then ends up coming to America to become (of all things) the Speaker of the House

(not to mention the lover of a single mom known only as "Hotsie"), *You Cannot Polish a Kurd* is in reality about the artifice of art—artifice that sits smug in its formulae, personae, dicta, and dogma until someone with Mr. Cork's skill and courage tears off the bath towel and laughs at its modest endowments.

Just as you begin to get involved in the plot, Cork mercilessly destroys it; as you begin to marvel at the stylized dialogue, Cork dispatches it by making all of his characters speak with exactly the same cadences and affectations: a mélange dialect sitting somewhere in the nexus of trekkie, surf-nazi, and alt rock DJ. A measure of Cork's genius is that we do not simply laugh at his characters, but at characterization itself, and the attempts—doomed to futility—to achieve it convincingly behind a proscenium.

And he has assembled a company of professional craftspersons who are all in on the same adroit joke. The director of the production as well as the author of the play, Cork has hired actors and design professionals who *get it*. From the actors who satirize "acting technique" to lighting artists who leave entire scenes in the dark while instruments focus on a downstage potted cactus holding, in its needles, a papier-mâché model of war-torn Iraq, Cork's ensemble dares the audience to see beyond the stale conventions of the theatre and their own minds and to imagine what representation would be like if the reality it represented were as artificial as the representation itself.

Whoa. And this afternoon I went out and got these new shades with round glass like Lennon used to wear.

FAME
by Desmond Cork—*July 17*

Not a good night last night, cats. The Babecat put on these shiny kind of underpants that got me all excited but then she slammed the door in my face just as I was getting on my knees.

See I'm kind of a celebrity here in Belverton now that my play *You Cannot Polish a Kurd* is getting rave reviews and all kinds of smart cats in glasses and tucked-in shirts with buttons are showing up to see its radical representism and whatnot.

Well cats let me tell you from the mouth du horse being a celeb is not all laughing with Jay and Dave by the pool. Truth, dudes? I haven't laughed with any celebs anywhere. I've been a celeb here in Belverton for like a week now and I haven't even laughed with my first has-been yet. And now I'm on the outs with the Babecat because of this little article they wrote on page six of the *Belverton Rat*.

> And guess who Yours Truly caught escorting Ms. **Candy Caress** to the Belverton University Midsummer Sex Symposium? That's right! None other than Belverton's own **Desmond Cork**, author and director of the critically acclaimed smash hit now

playing at the **Board Treaders Theatre** on Veblen Street. Candy was wearing a mesh gown over a lovely leather corset. Mr. Cork, dressed in a tuxedo t-shirt, entered with Ms. Caress on his arm—and walked right into a doorjamb! "Whoa," he said when he got up again. "I dropped like Curly! Guess I should wait 'til I sit down before checking out the fashion."

Note to Des: If you make it through the symposium, maybe Candy will let you "check out the fashion" at your own pace!

So the Babecat reads this and puts on these bull's-eye underpants that get me all steely and then lets me sleep out on the ol' sofa again like she did the night I showed her where Hotsie called her a hag.

So like cause of that little article I never got to check out *any* fashion at my own pace. Fame is *harsh*.

RETURN TO DR. WHARTON-STONE
by Barry Fest—*July 30*

Two days ago I received welcome news. My beloved wife, Dr. Wharton-Stone, rang me up at the office and told me I was free to return home. She rang off before I could give her my heartfelt thanks for ending my exile, during which four months (a seeming eon) I have lived here, in my office at the Belverton University Press.

It had been an uncomfortable, torturous, nay, *horrifying* exile. Not only did weak-tongue-induced headaches plague me, but my clothes and the office furniture were slowly befouling with the organic aromas of Chinese food, sleep sweat, and exfoliating Fest.

I had to break the news gently to Moliere, who had become accustomed to staying late with me and regaling me with tales of debauchery from her dormitory days. She taught me a completely new American idiom that she insists is in general usage by campus youth. (For instance, in this peculiar argot it is entirely possible to "give" one's "head" without prior decapitation!)

When Moliere came into my office that afternoon I noticed that the pink portion of her hair had been reduced to a streak amid the greenish blonde. Her skirt was the usual tulle, and over her massive dragon tattoo she wore a simple black t-shirt with the words WIVES CRY in white letters across the front.

When I gave her the news of my imminent return to Dr. Wharton-Stone, she only smiled and squinted at me. "So," she said, "no more late-night noodlin'?"

"I'm afraid not," I said as I arranged my pewter tea set in its wooden carrying box for transport back to Casa Fest.

"But tonight I was gonna show you how to tie a slip-knot with a black satin scarf."

I stopped packing for a moment. I had always regretted quitting the Boy Scouts before getting to the knots.

I shook my head. "No," I said. "We have the Press picnic coming up. Why, we'll have it down by the lake, and you can show me these knots with actual ropes connected to skiffs and sloops and what have you. What say you, Moliere?"

She continued simply grinning and looking in my eyes. She ran her finger down my forearm, the curious thing, then abruptly twisted her torso and turned for the door.

She was almost out of my office when she stopped and turned to me again. "Don't forget your tongue exerciser," she smiled.

It was a good thing she reminded me, because in my car on the way home I began to experience another, piercing headache. Cursing the biological curiosity, conundrum, nay, *enigma* connecting my tongue to my temples, I pulled over to the side of the road and reached into the stack of boxes on the back seat. I pulled out the red ball and strapped it to my face.

I am fortunately able to *multitask*, as Moliere likes to say, so I was able—without much difficulty—to steer the car while repeatedly pressing the ball with my tongue. I was on my third "set" of fifty "reps" when I turned the car into the driveway of my home—*my* home, my missed and cherished home, the home where I wear bedclothes to bed, the home where the furniture I lie upon whilst I sleep is not visible from the furniture I sit upon as I work.

I got out of the car and made my way up the flagstone walk to the small, side door of my house. My next-door neighbor, a man named Gromalion, was wearing a pith helmet and short white pants, watering his hedge, and smoking a cigarette.

When he saw me he laughed smoke through pursed lips.

"Hey, Fest," he said. "Forget your leash?"

"I have weak tongue, imbecile!" I shouted. Owing to the red ball, however, the effect of my outburst on Gromalion was limited to a series of muffled sounds, on the order of, "Mm-hm wmtm ym mm-b-smm!"

Gromalion took another drag of his fetid death stick. "Hey," he said again. "Didn't your wife teach you not to talk with your mouth full?"

He laughed in vulgar little hisses, again spewing smoke through his pursed lips. I turned away without another word. What did this moron know of weak tongue and headaches? I vowed to remain intrepid; to tend to my malady without regard to who might point at me and snicker. I am, after all, a radical, and have the monographs to prove it.

I entered the house through the side door that opened into the kitchen, and found Dr. Wharton-Stone seated at the table in a beige t-shirt and browsing the DSM-III.

Upon seeing me, she jumped.

I quickly unhooked the straps and spit out the red ball. "Do not be frightened, dearest," I said. "This is what they call a 'tongue exerciser.' I have weak tongue."

"*Tongue exerciser?*" she barked. "It's a ball gag, you chucklehead!"

"Ball...gag?"

"Yes," she said. "Ball gag. Sadomasochistic perverts—"

She cut herself off, flipped a few pages in the DSM, then

looked back up at me. "Sadomasochistic deviants and bored yuppies use it to play roles conducive to the psychogenic—"

She cut herself off again and gasped.

"Oh my God," she said, and cupped her hands over her mouth. She removed the hands slowly and said steadily: "That little Goth slut gave it to you, didn't she?"

"You mean Moliere?"

"Oh my God...she did, didn't she?"

"Yes, dear, she did. But before you judge the lass too harshly—"

"Barry," she said, her voice dripping with desperate pity, morbid disgust, or the true love of a true-loving lover, "can't you tell that this tattooed lust-hole sent you here wearing that thing just to make a fool of me?"

"Dear," I said, reassuringly, "why would a lust-hole waste her time trying to increase the stamina of my tongue?"

She shook her head and closed her eyes. "I can barely stand to look at you," she said.

I took that as an implicit re-imposition of exile. I turned slowly for the door, tongue-exerciser in hand.

"Where are you going?" I heard her voice behind me, as forbidding as the click of a pistol hammer.

"Back to the office, dearest."

"Oh...no...you...are...*not!*"

I turned to face her again. Her eyes flashed fire. She folded her arms. "You're staying here. You will go upstairs and put on your jammies."

"But...beloved, what about dinner?"

"I'll bring you in some cereal when I come up, little man," she snarled. "You're going to get into bed, where I can keep a leg across you."

So I trudged up the stairs, tongue exerciser in hand, wondering if Moliere had indeed sent me knowingly into this trap.

Moliere...I wonder what that musky smell is that I find so strong on her?

A CREDENTIAL
by Nefertiti Snorkjutt—*August 7*

Well, thanks to some of my students, I have discovered a travesty—well, perhaps not a travesty, but at least an *annoyance*—on the Internet.

That annoyance is seated—well, *occupies*—a part of the Internet I think they call *newsgroups*. A rumor is spreading there about, well, *me*, and I believe it is time that I extinguished it.

Here's what I'm talking about:

> On 4 Aug 23:30:25 GMT, lamprey@mcofilter.com wrote:
> \>\>OK, I've been hearing a lot of really weird stuff about those folks over
> \>\>at the
> \>\>Belverton University Press. Consider: the main
> \>\> woman over there,
> \>\>a feminist and academic named Nefertiti Snorkjutt (she's also an
> \>\>obvious
> \>\>secularist) was really into some shall we say *kinky* things in the 90s.
> \>\>Can anyone confirm?
> \>\>--Lamprey

Mmmm. I think I can confirm. I have some friends who lived in Chelsea (NYC) in the 80s, and they told me Snorkjutt was a pretty well-known freak. There was this one time—I don't *think* this is apocryphal, but take it for what it's worth—that the cops raided this club called Queen's Pleasure on the third floor of some 22nd Street crackerbox, and chased her and some other freaks down a fire escape. Snorkjutt climbed in the window of the theatre one floor down. (The window was in one of the dressing rooms.) She ran out onto the stage wearing a leather bustier and precious little else and was cuffed while looking for an exit.
—Brian

Well, there *may* have been an incident with a small theatre and a bustier. (I seem to remember some very bright lights and looking for an aisle through an audience, but sometimes I think that was just a dream I had.)

It should not come, at least, I don't *think* it should come as any surprise that—before I was recognized as an academic expert on the subject of reforming misogynists—I did some field research on the subject.

I don't know what you would call it, but I have always thought of it as a credential.

EATING RAMONES
by Desmond Cork—*August 14*

Hey cats! Rock scholarship is catching on at last! Every day I'm Googling to see if they're quoting me on MTV.com or that other one VH1.com and oh yeah Wikipedia.
(Nothing yet cats.)
And like I'm sacrificing for the cause. The Babecat wants to make out, yeah? She keeps patting the empty space on the bed next to her and arching her back like she wants to use my bod to burn some loose estro but I just rebuckle and scamper. Rock scholarship doesn't take time out to flash nasty.

So like while I was working with these cats who were putting on my play—*You Cannot Polish a Kurd*—and becoming a local celeb and whatnot, the ol' inbox filled up with a ton of letters and most of them are pretty worthy. But the one I'm answering tonight is most important for especially you younger kids to grok because it touches on the two things you have to know if you want to know anything about the music scene. Namely the Ramones and the estro conspiracy.
Here it is:

Hi Des.

My name is Sandra. How ya doin'? Listen. Got a question for you. I was wondering if you could tell me what happened to the original Ramones. You know, Joey, Johnny, Dee Dee, and Tommy. Because like...OK, here's the thing. I keep hearing that Tommy? You know. I keep hearing that Tommy is the last of the original Ramones. So what happened to the other ones?

Oh, and like, OK, I know that their last name wasn't really Ramone. Could you tell me what they were? Their real last names, I mean?

Thanks,
Sandra

Okay this chick Sandra? She's a victim cats. A victim of the fake truth the estro establishment has put out on the Ramones. See what they don't teach in the high schools? (And if you've ever been in like a teacher's lounge cats you know it's all about estro in there.) Is that Joey and Johnny and Dee Dee and Tommy were *not* the original Ramones. The *original* original Ramones were Rutger and Elmer and Scam and Privy.

And *their* real last name was *Ramone*.

Who on the New York punk scene could forget Rutger who wore the low-rise jeans and who thought he could talk to the sky if it was a really clear day? Or Elmer the lyrics-writing cat who wrote the first rock opera that had no words in it except for "yeah" and "c'mon"?

And who can forget Scam who had that day job selling shingles? Or Privy who was an undisputed something?

Who can forget? I'll tell you dudes: *everyone*. The original original Ramones have just disappeared from rock memory.

What happened to them? Why doesn't anyone outside of official rock scholarshipdom know? Why the ol' cover up?

Simple. It's because what happened to the original original Ramones is one of the grossest acts in the history of rock—

and estro. So like you may want to shield your eyes and have your mom read the next sentence to you kind of slow. Ready? *The Ramones were eaten alive by four girls who later on turned into the Donnas.*

No crap cats. It was a tragedy of seriously huge tragicality. See the Ramones didn't have to worry too much about the estro crazies when nobody knew who they were, but one night at Max's Kansas City they were playing "Yeah C'mon" and these chicks with really wide eyes wearing these skirts made of their own hair charged the stage and carried Privy off to the ladies' room. (Which is how he got his name by the way.)

They got so scared they decided to leave New York for a while (Max's Kansas City is *not* in Missouri, cats) to tour Southern California. They were playing to a sold-out crowd at the Grok This! festival in Redondo Beach when these four teenage babes came up to them after and told the Ramones that they could eat them raw.

Well cats, there was no way the original original Ramones could know this meant they were going to end up served like sushi on seaweed to a bunch of estro junkies so they followed these chicks home and like never came back. In L.A. they say you can still hear Scam and Privy laughing down the canyons whenever one of the Donnas ralphs.

Okay well I know what some of you stickler cats are going to say. You're going to say, "Des. Dude. How could the Donnas be old enough to have eaten the original original Ramones and still look as young as they do? I mean they look like they're in their twenties. Why don't they look older? What's their secret?"

Are you listening dudes? Their secret is *eating Ramones*.

AN INTERVIEW WITH SLAPPY GOERING
by Nefertiti Snorkjutt—*August 21*

If you have been read—well, *keeping up*, you know that I am investigating—well, perhaps not investigating but at least *analyzing*—the presidential campaign of Reformed Misogyny Party candidate, Congressman Slappy Goering (a former comedian who is also deep).

Goering is also the only major candidate to promise not to get an erection before Election Day. (Unfortunately his running mate, Stiv Corkman—the actor who played the pig's head in the 1990 remake of *Lord of the Flies*—has so far resisted making a similar pledge.)

A few days after he agreed to be interviewed by me, I found myself (well, I didn't exactly *find* myself but I at least *appeared*) in a small den at Goering Campaign headquarters here in Belverton. The only other person in there at the time was, well, a *woman* whom I took to be a campaign aide dressed in a smart suit. She was sitting on a small sofa near a smaller, well, *couch*. Her hands were folded like currency in her lap, and she had the look of a feral child.

"So how long have you worked for the congressman?" I said into the microphone of my tape recorder.

I put the, um, well, I *extended* the microphone to her, expecting an answer.

She stared at it.

I rewound and played my voice asking her the question again. She giggled and put her finger in her mouth.

"Tapey," she whispered.

At that point Goering and his pig-faced running mate entered. Pig-face was wearing a wrinkled sports jacket and a green novelty tie with a shamrock on it. A gold shamrock. He smiled at me a pink-gummed smile, a lathered smile, a smile that wanted to know the taste of my rump. (A girl can tell.)

Goering, a fiftyish, handsome man with curly black hair, wore a black suit and what looked, at first glance, like a matching skirt and leggings. But a second look showed that it was a spac—well, *unusual* pair of pants very spacious at the hips. Pants that I think you could say *billowed* from the knees to the waist, like a pair of jodhpurs five sizes too large for a man three times his size.

"Snorkety!" he cried when he saw me, and extended his hand. I shook it, staring all the while into his reddish, grinning face. "I see you met wifety!" He pointed to the idiot on the sofa and sat next to her.

"Wifey-poo," she giggled.

I turned on the recorder. "Let's get to it," I said.

"Nyuk! Nyuk! Nyuk!" he said.

What follows is the transcript of our interview:

> *Snorkjutt*: I couldn't help noticing your pants when you walked in.
>
> *Goering*: That's what all the femfolk say.
>
> *Pig-Face*: Rimshot!
>
> *Snorkjutt*: But seriously, how can we be expected to know whether you are breaking your campaign

promise in those pants? I mean, well, *really*, who can tell whether you have an erection or not?

Goering: Let's ask my wife! Cindy, daddum packum woodum?

Idiot: No woodum, daddum!

Goering: See? And if I get one, she'll be the first to go run and tell the media.

Snorkjutt: All right, I'll, well, *stipulate* your flaccidity.

Goering: Thanx mucho incalculado. You see, a Goering presidency will dispel the myth that women want men for sex. That will be my top priority. You see, the greatest problem facing society today is the woman's fear of being thought of in that way.

Snorkjutt: Do you agree with the, well, *premise* that men are from Mars and women are from Venus?

Goering: I disagree with that position, but only because its advocates do not go far enough.

Snorkjutt: Oh really?

Goering: That's right. You see, women are not just from Venus, they are from an obscure, penis-hating crater on Venus. Men, on the other hand, are from Singapore and Titian.

Snorkjutt: Singapore and Titian?

Goering: Sing a poor rendition of *what?* Nyuk! Nyuk! Nyuk!

Snorkjutt: What is your position on the Defense of Marriage Act? Do you think gays should be allowed to marry?

Goering: I believe that marriage is between a man and a woman—no, wait. I believe that man is between a marriage and a woman. Whoa, whoa, whoa. I think it's woman is between man and the Super Bowl.

Pig-face: Rimshot!

Goering: Nyuk! Nyuk! Nyuk! Men should love women with the same kind of affection they can honestly say they feel for the shortstop of their favorite baseball team. You know, not love based on physical...watchit! But based on a person's ability to handle little white balls with a cowhide glove.

Snorkjutt: It is so, well, *refreshing* to hear a politician say that!

Goering: For instance, when I look at you, I don't see a *woman*, I see a *person*. A person who happens to have spectacular breasts and a pair of hips that are begging to bear my children.

Snorkjutt: Trust me, Congressman, if we ever got together there would be plenty of begging, but not from my side of the room.

Goering: Exactly.

Snorkjutt: Huh?

Goering: That's why a Goering presidency will insist on legislation that creates erection-free zones, where women can be sure they will not behold men in a state of…watchit!

Snorkjutt: But what do you say—well, perhaps not *say*, but what do you *rejoin* when critics say that other countries have tried the same thing by forcing women to wear burkhas?

Goering: A Goering presidency will not insist on burkhas. I think we're a little more enlightened than that, here in the West. I think women should wear what they want and, if necessary, men should be required to magic-marker their eyeballs to keep from seeing anything that might arouse them in the physical sense. A Goering presidency will acknowledge that *real* men never wanted orgasms to begin with…

Snorkjutt: Really?

Goering: Watchit!

Idiot: Woodum!

I think that, well, I *hope* that you can agree with me when I say that Congressman Slappy's heart is in the right place, even if he is a little confused over what sort of wife can command his, well, *obedience*. Isn't it ironic that, well, even our deeper former comedians consort with dips?

As Goering left the room, I wasn't sure, but I thought I could see something swaying in his trousers, giving the overall impression of a mizzenmast fore.

Pig-face snorted and winked when he saw what I was looking at, making me think that the whole, um, *Goering* Campaign could endure closer scrutiny, before even one woman's vote is wasted.

I may have to go under, well, *cover*.

THE PUBLIC VEGETARIAN
by Desmond Cork—*August 28*

Hey cats. Lousy week for the ol' Des. The Babecat moved out and took most of her stuff.

I'm like trying not to take it personally? But it's hard not to be kind of down. I mean maybe she just needs some space but like it could be she hates my guts. Here's what went down cats, and like it's a matter of principle.

It's just that when I go out to eat in public? Then I never eat anything that used to be a part of an animal. When I'm eating in though I pretty much scarf anything that didn't used to be a person especially if they used to be a single mom or one of those cats who sit on the sidewalk and have these magic marker signs that say why their life sucks. See, those little round turkeys in the plastic packs are already dead. I feel sorry for them and all? But mmmmm...white meat.

The Babecat is like a *real* meat-eater though, and she does it in restaurants where people at the other tables can see she just doesn't care about the ol' animals. And the Babecat? She doesn't care that other people can see she doesn't care and that's like heartless.

So last week we're at this restaurant near campus called Edgar's. (It's got one of those tickets right near the front door that says the government comes in and makes sure the kitchen's clean. That always makes me feel better, cats.)

Like I said we're eating there and she orders the roast beef even though she knows how much I hate it when people eat meat in front of people. So I'm like sitting there thinking, "What would Greenpeace do?" and when she's done I pick up her plate and throw the gravy on her jeans.

I was trying to be educational and whatnot? But the Babecat got real mad about it.

Then last Wednesday I got home from ye ol' Johnny Thunders Memorial Library where I do most of my rock scholarship and the Babecat was gone and so was most of her stuff which includes this big sofa I like to nap in. There was a note in her handwriting that said: "BYE, DUDE! Mom and Dad came to get me? And we're going out to scarf BURGERS!"

Whoa. Public burger-scarfing. That is *way* against my principles cats. I was kind of down? But I was also kind of hungry so I went out to the market and got some of that happening ground beef and cooked up some burgers in private and scarfed them at home.

I know what you're thinking, cats. I feel sorry for those cows and all but they were dead long before I got to the market.

PIG B
by Desmond Cork—*September 4*

Okay cats, so I was like really upset about the Babecat moving out and taking all her stuff, including that big sofa I like to nap in. And all because I'm a public vegetarian with public-vegetarian principles which means I had to throw some gravy on her pants.

Well just a couple days later the Babecat calls me back (I was pretty much calling her every hour or so except at night) and says, "Des. Dude. I've been thinking about it, dude. I'm down with the whole vegetarian nasty? But you can't be a vegetarian only in public. If it means anything you have to stop eating meat in private, too."

I had like gross reservations about that last part cats, but I'm thinking, "Okay don't judge. One step at a time. Easy does it. Today is the first day of the rest of the Babecat's life."

So the Babecat rolls back to the apt without her sofa (she like had to have it delivered in a truck or something) and right away she goes to the fridge and starts trashing everything with an Oscar or a Mayer on it and I'm like watching close and saying over and over real low to myself, "Don't judge don't judge don't judge…"

But like if I'm not judging her and she's wrong then I'm thinking she probably won't judge me either especially with me being right and whatnot. So I go out that night to the market and I get a pack of that happening salami—just enough for a single plug—and the Babecat goes WMD on me.

So I'm explaining to her that you know nothing I do is going to bring this pig back. I didn't want to make it too hard to understand since she's new to the whole public-vegetarian scene but then she says: "Des. Dude. Don't you know that if you eat Pig A they have to kill Pig B to take her place, dude?"

I know that sounds like way off cats but she really said it. So I'm like, "Babecat, not to pull rank or anything? But I used to be a stock boy in a market and I never saw anybody kill Pig B. I mean that just doesn't go down."

Then she says real patient which I guess is good but kind of irks me anyway: "Des. Dude. They don't kill Pig B at the market, dude. They order from the wholesaler. The wholesaler orders from the slaughterhouse. They do the killing at the slaughterhouse. It's like remote control."

Whoa. I didn't understand any of that so instead of arguing? I started oinking to lighten things up. I mean life's too short for an attitude, yeah?

So she moved out again. And I'm thinking now I really have to buy my own sofa.

MY "BODYGUARD"
by Barry Fest—*September 11*

I have already referred to the strange goings-on in my life as a "rollercoaster ride." Indeed, I am becoming somewhat defensive, frightened, alienated, nay, *paranoid*. It seems to me at all times that I am being watched by the ubiquitous individual known to the Woodstock Generation as The Man.

My elegant, educated, and intellectual wife—Dr. Wharton-Stone—has become obsessively jealous of Moliere, the Belverton University Press's exotic email administrator, whom she calls "that Goth bitch." Indeed, last month she resolved to keep me at home, in bed, with her leg strapped across my chest—all to ensure that I do not wander off to some rendezvous with Moliere, who possesses a musky scent I have always found attractive on women, even though I cannot place the source of said scent precisely.

I spent three nights trapped under Dr. Wharton-Stone's left thigh, and three days confined by her to my house and grounds. (How, you may ask, did she find the means to confine me, a grown man and a radical? The answer is as simple as it is terrible, my friends. She glowered. And Dr. Wharton-Stone's glowerings are portents of unspecified, but always grave, ills.—Ills I no longer wear the bravado to brook.)

So I sat about my home, communicating with my office by means of a computer "remote," which one of the morlocks had come to "hook up" for me. I managed to answer my glMail, imagining, as I did so, our glMail administrator—the tingle-inducing Moliere—smiling as she saw the little missives appear in, then disappear from, my outbox.

Although my confinement induced in me a moribund funk at first, I soon realized, to my satisfaction, that it actually opened up fresh opportunities. Indeed, I was now able to finish household chores that had long been awaiting my spare time.—Time that I now had in abundance. The thermostat on the cellar furnace had been broken for months, so I finally sat myself down and wrote the monograph, "Thermostat: The Broken Promise of Automation," and sent it off via glMail to the editors of *Fishhook Salad*, the literary quarterly.

I was at work on the long-overdue and long-awaited combination of the names "Obama" and "Clinton" as part of my quadrennial foray into satire. I had tried and jettisoned "Clintama" and "Obinton," and was entertaining "Amanton" and "Clioba" when the doorbell sounded.

I dawdled a bit more over the names, laughing, I must admit, at an ingenuity that surprises even me sometimes, when Dr. Wharton-Stone ushered in a shortish, dark-haired man with a brush mustache. He wore a beige sports jacket with patches at the elbows, matching pants, and loafers. His white shirt looked unpressed, as did his thin, black-and-yellow striped tie.

"This is Mickey," Dr. Wharton-Stone said, as if I should understand, without being told, that his last name was either Mouse or Rooney. "He's from an agency that's done some work for me before."

"What work was that, dearest?" I had the impudence to ask.

She glowered me to a gasp. "He doesn't talk much...or at all," she went on, "but he did get some superior recommendations."

At that precise moment I noticed a sparkle in Mickey's eye. I am not making metaphors. A spark of light *twinkled* in his right eye. His mouth, under the mustache, turned up in an unmistakable smile. It was...likable, amiable, endearing, nay, *affable*.

He removed a pad from the breast pocket of his jacket and began jotting notes in it with a cheap blue pen.

"You can go back to work, if you want—and anyplace else you like—as long as Mickey accompanies you at all times," Dr. Wharton-Stone said.

"Thank you, my darling. Does that mean he has to stay in my office with me? Or may I seat him in a cubicle with the morlocks?"

She glowered again, and I knew, via the nonverbal communication that accompanies the bond between man and wife, that Mickey would be at my side—if not seated in my lap—for as long as Dr. Wharton-Stone felt threatened by the sultry and ingratiating Moliere.

I turned to Mickey. "Do you have a last name, or shall I call you Mr. Mickey?" I asked.

He smiled, took his right arm out of his elbow-patched sports jacket, and rolled his shirtsleeve up almost to his shoulder revealing the curled, green serpent's tail that constituted the tattoo on his upper arm.

"Ah," I said. "Your name is Serpenttail?"

His grin lost none of its affability as he shook his head. But I admit I was at a loss. "Ophidiantail?" I guessed again.

"Snaketail," said Dr. Wharton-Stone with dead certainty.

Mickey nodded and tapped his nose.

"Your name is Mickey Snaketail?" I asked. He nodded and re-dressed his arm. "All right, I suppose then you are my…bodyguard?" He nodded yet again, tapped his nose, and made a note in his little memo pad.

"Don't you even own a PDA?" Dr. Wharton-Stone asked. "I hope you don't expect *me* to transcribe those notes!"

Mickey shook his head and jotted something down on a blank page. When he turned it to us, this is what we saw:

I HAD A LAPTOP LEFT IT IN MAUI

Dr. Wharton-Stone shook her head contemptuously. Mickey looked confused.

"Shouldn't there be a semicolon between 'laptop' and 'left'?" I asked.

Mickey scribbled quickly, then showed us the pad again.

KURT VONNEGUT HATES SEMICOLONS

Dr. Wharton-Stone stood stock-still and stared. "Oh my God," she whimpered. "I *love* Kurt Vonnegut!"

She stared into his eyes for a moment, then leapt up and kissed him on the cheek. Just a peck, but a peck from Dr. Wharton-Stone is practically third base.

"Barry," she said as she turned to me, "no more semicolons."

"Noted," I said.

And with that, Mickey and I left for the office.

THE FINING LIFESTYLE
by Desmond Cork—*September 18*

Hey cats. So I keep calling the Babecat's parents' house to talk her into coming back to me and whatnot. (She split and took the sofa I like to nap in.) I've been leaving messages on her machine? And she's been like screening me out except for this one time when her old man came on and told me to like go to hell.

Then I got home Friday and found this message on my answering machine. It's from the Babecat's old man. (I put little stars in the curses so like if you're pure and whatnot? You won't have to look at a bunch of words that might make you into a pervert one day.)

> Desmond, G** d*** it! If you call my f***ing house one more f***ing time I'm going to get one of the darts off my lawn and come over and shove it up your corduroy-coated a**!
>
> Can I ask you a question? And don't call me back to answer it, you stupid a**h***. Are you such a g** d*** f***ing idiot that you don't know when you've been f***ing dumped? Now Lola's living at home and she's a f***ing vegetarian thanks to you!

And you don't even do it right! You stupid son of a b****! Now my wife is into it, and I've got tofu coming out of my a**!

The Babecat's old man doesn't know a whole lot of swear words, yeah? But the ones he does know he uses a lot. Cause like in that little message he curses me out twelve times.

So I got this great idea, cats. Just before I picked up that message I was reading about that time when the FCC fined Howard Stern $27,500 for each racial and sexual nasty he said on the air and at first I'm like, "Whoa, is Howard about freedom of speech? Or is he just about hate speech, yeah?" And then when I heard the Babecat's old man cursing me out it hit me. Fining is a pretty good idea and it's maybe something I should be doing. Like a lifestyle.

So I figured it out. Twelve curse words times $27,500 is a real lot of money, dudes. So I sent the Legal Aid dude a copy of the message tape and he's sending the Babecat's old man the fine.

I mean I'm still bummed and all because the Babecat split? But if you turn up Bad Religion really loud and stare at a stack of dollar bills you can forget a real lot of harsh.

MOLIERE'S LICKED FIST
by Barry Fest—*September 25*

Oh, my friends, it has been an interesting, compelling, nay, *fascinating* few weeks. In my last entry I described my introduction to Mickey Snaketail, the affable—but mute—companion assigned me by my wife, Dr. Wharton-Stone. In the company of a chaperone is the only way Dr. Wharton-Stone will permit me to leave the grounds of our shared domicile, so great is her fear that I may fall prey to the lusts of our gothic glMail administrator, Moliere.

Mickey sat beside me in the car on that first drive to the office, watching—with the intensity of a cat stalking a feather in the breeze—everything we passed on the street, as if it were his first time in Belverton or in a moving vehicle. He craned his neck to see the GOERING FOR PRESIDENT posters hanging in Guevara Square. "You look like a veritable Alice surveying Wonderland," I volunteered. He wrote something with his blue plastic pen in the little pad he always carried with him.

When he was done he turned the pad to me, and I read his message out of the corner of my eye as I drove.

HOW DID YOU END UP NEEDING A CHAPERONE

I told him about Moliere, the tongue-exerciser she gave me, and Dr. Wharton-Stone's fear that Moliere wanted me in the naughty way.

Mickey nodded.

"An old story, is it?" I asked.

He nodded again.

"What you may not know, for I have not volunteered this even to my loving wife, is that Moliere possesses a musky, titillating, nay, *funky* smell, to use the campus vernacular."

Mickey scribbled.

TELL ME MORE

"It is a smell I have always found attractive on women.— As if they had just come from the gymnasium without showering...*completely*."

Mickey made a note. I glanced over, but he did not show it to me.

I shrugged.

"I feel a headache coming on, Mr. Snaketail. Could you do me a favor and place the tongue-exerciser on my face? I believe it is on the back seat."

He found the *objet* in question and fastened the red ball firmly, but not painfully, in my mouth. We continued in silence to the office.

Once there, I removed the tongue-exerciser, placed it in the top drawer of my office desk, and summoned Moliere. I did not want to confront the lass too harshly, but I wanted to know—nay, I *needed* to know—if the tongue-exerciser was in fact the nefarious ball-gag Dr. Wharton-Stone insisted it was.

When she arrived in my office she was wearing the usual ankle-length, tulle skirt, and a black t-shirt with the words GO SOUTH YOUNG MAN in white letters across the chest.

Mickey was seated beside my desk. Moliere stared at the stranger as she sat in the gray, felt-covered chair in front of me.

"Who's the newbie?" she asked.

I explained.

Moliere smiled and relaxed, draping one of her legs languorously over the arm of her chair. "Your chaperone, huh? Interesting…"

Mickey chuckled soundlessly, giving me the bizarre sense of watching a man sneeze inside a telephone booth.

Moliere watched him with furrowed brow, then turned to me. "What's his deal?" she asked. "Your wife got his tongue?"

Mickey ceased his chuckling and thrust his tongue through his meaty lips, presumably to demonstrate that Dr. Wharton-Stone did not have it on her person.

Moliere giggled.

"Hey, boss, whaddaya say we give him the ol' fist test?" she asked.

Before I could pronounce yea or nay, she thrust her fist sideways into Mickey's face. "Try pryin' my fist open with your tongue, Snaketail," she challenged.

Mickey placed his tongue in the side of her fist. I felt a violent urge to look away, as I knew he was doomed to humiliation. Fascination overcame trepidation, however, and my eyes were riveted on the two of them. Mickey began working his tongue, remarkably, between her fingers. I expected him to quit at any moment, provoking Moliere to giggles, but instead I witnessed a gargantuan struggle of wills as the muscles in Mickey's bull neck rippled and Moliere leaned forward, her whole body vibrating as she fought to keep her fist clamped tight.

A few moments later, Moliere's quivering fingers were splayed apart. She sank back into the gray chair, wide-eyed and panting. "Nice…" she said finally, wiping her hand on her t-shirt.

Mickey gave her a modest shrug.

"Wow," she continued. "I bet that tongue can untie wet rope."

There was a pause as Moliere stared at Mickey, her palpable awe distilling to esteem. I found myself jealous.

"Um?" I interrupted. They indulged me with a glance. "I think you should know that I have been doing my tongue exercises on a regular basis, Moliere. Indeed, Mickey witnessed my tongue flexion on our way to the office this morning."

Mickey corroborated with a series of quick nods.

"Let's check it out, boss," Moliere said.

The test was upon me. She leaned across the desk and put her sideways fist into my face. She smiled. Emboldened by Mickey's triumph, I licked my lips and thrust my doughty tongue into the center.

But I failed. I think, at some point, I felt that I was making headway, but in the end all I managed was to get her hand wet.

She patted my head like my name was Mittens. "Don't sprain it, boss," she said. "You're gonna need it!"

And with that she bounced out of the office, leaving me an image of myself damned to a velvet-lined hell, with succubae stroking me where the steel teeth of my zipper once meshed.

I turned to Mickey and stared deeply into his eyes. "I love my wife," I said.

He wrote it down.

THE BABECAT RETURNS
by Desmond Cork—*October 2*

Hey cats. Well it looks like fining the Babecat's old man for using all those curse words on my answering machine was the right idea in the right place. Here's what went down since last time.

Okay, first? This commissioners group or what have you that works for the government? They chimed in and said they weren't too keen on having a guy like me who doesn't have a badge going around and laying fines on cats for saying curse words on answering machines. But because the curse words were really bad and said on an answering machine like I said? If I reported it in then they would maybe fine the Babecat's old man themselves, which I guess is okay except then I don't get the money when he pays up.

So then the Babecat's old man called up my legal aid dude to see if he could get me to like not report him. But the legal aid dude got all steely on him and started saying words like "ill-advised" and "pursuant" so the Babecat's old man sent in the Babecat to see if she couldn't work it out where she would move back in with me if I would forget about telling on him.

Then we got in this confab with her legal aid dude and mine and we worked out this deal. And like the Babecat's legal aid dude really groks the lawyering cats. He got a few things into the deal that mean I have to do some extra stuff

and my lawyer kind of looked out the window and yawned and didn't fight back at all and when I gave him my what-up? look he just said "Hey, you want the couch back or what?" And I'm like: "Digital."
So here's a few sentences from the paper I signed.

> Herein it is agreed by DESMOND CORK ("Desmond") and LOLA WILDE ("Lola") that Lola will return to, and continue to reside at, 213 Wingwood Street, Apartment 4A, the premises of which shall be shared by Lola and Desmond equally. On her return, Lola shall restore the big sofa, which is described in detail in Addendum A.
>
> In return, Desmond agrees to withdraw any and all complaints, reports, or assertions he may have made to any and all agencies of the United States Government ("the Government") and to forego any and all future complaints, reports, or assertions to any and all agencies of the Government, regarding Lola's father WALTER WILDE ("Walter") for Walter's use of obscene language in the telephone message transcribed in Addendum B. Desmond further promises that he will be a vegetarian in public and private, that he will not hide, smuggle, or secret meat, that he will not begin to fall asleep while Lola is speaking or check his watch during consortium, which consortium shall be defined as any period of time beginning with heavy petting and continuing until Lola pushes Desmond away or leaves the room.

Some stiff conditions, yeah? But the Babecat is back and so is her sofa. I'm looking right at it and screaming for a nap, cats. And my lawyer says if I can nod off before the Babecat starts talking or kissing me I won't be breaking any rules.

SLAPPY GOERING CONCEDES
by Nefertiti Snorkjutt—*November 5*

I think, well, I *guess* you must have heard on the news by now that Slappy Goering did *not* win the, well, *presidential election*.

Who is the *real* Slappy Goering, you ask? Well, he is a congressman. A husband. He is a former comedian who is also deep. Over the past several weeks I have come to know—well, perhaps not *know*, but at least become *acquainted with* Congressman Slappy and his wife, as well as Slappy's running mate Stiv Corkman (the actor who played the pig's head in the 1990 remake of *Lord of the Flies*), and his escort.

Congressman Slappy ran on the Reformed Misogyny ticket, and was the only candidate who promised not to get an erection before Election Day.

He is, well, a *genius*.

When I think of all the wonderful—well, perhaps not wonderful, but at least *terrific* stuff that would have sprung into existence had Slappy been given the chance he deserves, well, knowing that he lost just makes me want to cry. The rest of the world hates America. The unempowered are, well, *lacking empowerment*. The ecosystem has stopped growing plankton for the little fish, or has started growing too much (whatever). Gays are unmarried. Men are disobedient. Children point.

And all for want of Slappy!

I was with Slappy when the sad news was broad—well, *came*. He said nothing at first. He took the hand of his twenty-eight year-old wife and escorted her into a room to confer with her for an hour and forty five minutes. When he emerged he was smiling and wearing tight-fitting jeans in place of the baggy-crotched trousers that had become his campaign trademark.

Immediately he rang up Al Gore to confer with him on the best way to proceed legally. The woman on the other end of the line said that Mr. Gore was on his way to Starbucks to return an unsatisfactory latté and could not be reached at the moment.

He then called the winner, to offer his congratulations but was unable to get past the White House butler's—well, a *little girl* related to the White House serving staff. Slappy begged: "Can't I please just be president in Belverton? I won the Belverton vote!"—But the little bitch just laughed.

Finally, Slappy made the inevitable, heartrending concession speech to his followers here in Belverton University's Guevara Square. I have reprint—well, *transcribed* it below in its entirety.

> Thank you so much. Thank you, thank you. Nyuk! Nyuk! Nyuk! Thank you, thank you so much.
>
> Thank you so much. You just have no idea how great it is for a fifty-year-old man to be able to fit into a normal-sized pair of pants after six months of saltpeter and children's songs. I'm gratified by it.
>
> I spoke to the little girl who picked up the phone at the White House and I told her that I knew where she lived, and that kidnappers were on the way.
>
> Nyuk! Nyuk! Nyuk!

But seriously, we had a good conversation, and we talked about the danger of boredom in our country; and I conveyed to her how much fun—how much jolly good fun it can be to drop burning matches into a gasoline can you're pretty sure is dry.

And she assured me that today she would begin having that fun.

In Belverton, it is vital that every vote count, and that every vote be counted. And it is now clear that when all the votes *are* counted, which they will be, I will win Belverton.

But they say I cannot be president of Belverton. Something about it being against the law of the land.

Didja ever notice that whenever you want to try out a new idea, there's always somebody saying it's against the law of the land? Who started calling it the law of the *land*, anyway? Does that mean if we jump up off the ground the law doesn't apply to us anymore? If that's the case, then all Bill Clinton had to prove was that he had his feet on Monica's back. And what if it's the law of Neverland? Heck, I think the only law there was drink the Jesus Juice and tell Michael if you hear sirens.

Whoa. What is this, an audience or the chalk outline at Jonestown?

Nyuk! Nyuk! Nyuk!

But seriously, I wish that I could just wrap you up in my arms individually, like those slices of processed cheese food in my refrigerator. What's the deal with those, anyway? Are they afraid if the slices touch each other they'll be tainted somehow, like some sort of sick, dairy incest?

Now that's what I call lactose intolerance!

Nyuk! Nyuk! Nyuk!

Anyway, I will always be tremen-diddly-ous grateful to the colleague who became my partner, my very close friend, an extraordinary running mate, and a dead ringer for a pig's head, Stiv Corkman.

I thank him for everything he did—and a few things he didn't do, like make good on his promise to prove that the human rectum is a musical instrument.

Thank you, sir.

And just remember, in an American election, nobody ever really loses, because whether or not our candidates are successful, the next morning we all wake up Americans—usually with a tap on the shoulder and the words, "I feel frisky."

Nyuk! Nyuk! Nyuk!

The anachronistic American electoral system may have prevented Congressman Slappy from becoming president of Belverton, but he will always be president of, well, my *heart*.

TONGUE IS HUGE
by Desmond Cork—*November 9*

Okay something weird is going down with the Babecat. See, while I'm working hard on rock scholarship every night the Babecat is off doing stuff and like before? She used to be begging me to drop denim and flash nasty.

And then there's her phone. Every time it goes off she's diving for it. I was sitting right next to it last Sunday, and she was in the shower and it went off and I could hear bottles getting knocked over and thumping in the bathroom and I shout, "Hey Babecat! No sweat, yeah? I'll get it!"

But instead of saying, "Des! Dude! Thanks, dude!" she hauls out of there all wet and splashy and dives for it and like nearly breaks my hand and she gets me all wet and takes the phone back into the bathroom giggling her ass off to whoever's on the other end.

That's when this idea started coming to the front of my brain. It was this idea that said, "Des. Dude. What's up with the Babecat, dude?"

(Ideas in my brain sometimes talk like the Babecat now that she moved back in.)

Turns out she has a second day job in a deli and I didn't even know about it!

See a couple nights ago I'm in the living room reading the ol' rock scholarship email checking for worthy questions from you, my loyal public, who can't get straight answers from the estro establishment. I found this one that went like this:

Desmond,

I am writing to you from India. Not quite, I don't think, well, not quite in India proper but I will call it India for simplicity.

Here is my question for you. My friends and I at university have observed that Jerry Lee Lewis, Iggy Pop, and Woody Allen all have had sex with teenager girls. Not with the same teenager girls and I don't think they are having the sex still, but my friends and I at university would like to know, if this is against the law in the States, why it is not against the law for these three men. Or is it only rockers (I have seen it written even as "rawkers") and Woody Allen who are allowed to partake of your daughters?

Thank you,
Pankaj

Whoa. A question about our bounteous laws. I was about to tell the ol' Indian dude about how rockers (and I guess Woody Allen) can be victims of teen babes who're getting their first jolts of estro when the Babecat comes in all tricked out in a black vinyl skirt and thigh-high fishnets—and pacing like she was ready to throw herself on the sofa and bawl. Turns out she wanted to go out with one of her friends but they broke the little date.

Hey, I'm sitting there feeling kind of sorry for her 'cause I saw *Sex and the City* while they were showing it and I know how important it is for chicks to hang out and say things like "up the butt" sometimes. It makes them feel empowered like they have the same way with words we men have. See in the seventies? Only guys got to go to bars and say "up the butt."

Those were some evil times, dudes.

But the Babecat calmed down soon and changed into some gym pants and a sweatshirt with the arms ripped off and went into the bedroom with her phone and closed the door. I was cracking the rock books (it's okay to call them rawk books if you want) when I hear it go off with this ringtone that sounds like Bowie singing "wham-bam thank you ma'am!" in that way he does. A few seconds later I hear the Babecat giggling and then it gets all quiet for a while and I hear these sounds like sobbing or weeping. You know, like: "Oh…oh…"

Then I hear these little squeals? And they keep getting louder until she screams out: "Oh my God!"

When she came out she said it was her boss from her day job and he fired her.

"Whoa, Babecat," I said. "So you won't be signing people up at the health club tomorrow?"

Turns out she meant a different day job and that's when she told me she had this second day job—which I guess was actually a night job—at a deli.

"Hey Babecat," I said. "How does shifting in ye ol' deli square with your being a vegetarian?"

She stared real hard at my face for a second. Then she said, "Des. Dude. That's exactly it, dude. I tried to get them to change the deli to a veggie deli so they fired me."

"Whoa!" I shouted because now I was prickly mad. "I don't think they can do that, Babecat. I mean, I think it's against the law to fire someone in these modern eras of ours unless they ask if it's okay first. So like what did he say when he fired you?"

"Well, he said it was about the tongue."

"Tongue," I said. "Deli tongue. Tongue on a hook... tongue on rye can be tasty. That's what I remember anyway before I was a full-on vegetarian even in private."

"Yeah. Tongue on rye. Tasty. So he says, 'I need to speak to you, Ms. Wilde,' and I'm like, 'Okay,' and he's like, 'Ms. Wilde, I heard that you wanted to get rid of the tongue, you know, because you're a full-on vegetarian even in private but I'm afraid that's out of the question.' Then he says, 'In fact we're going to be using even *more* tongue at the deli.'"

"I get that," I said. "Tongue is huge."

"Right," she said. "So then he says, 'Ms. Wilde, I'm firing you over that tongue.' That got my juices running, Des, and then he says, 'And once I've got you fired we're going to do things with that tongue you never thought were even possible. We're going to serve it fresh on platters. We're going to dip it into soups for flavor. We're going to slice it nice and thick onto lettuce. And when we find something the customers really like we're going to just keep doing that again and again, slowly at first then—'"

"Babecat," I said. "Could you like cut to the chase? I have to tell some Indian dude why Iggy Pop humps teens."

"So he has a lot of new things planned for the tongue," she said, "and he knew it would drive me out of my mind."

"Whoa. Babecat. That is *harsh*, babe," I said. "That is some weird sadistic cat. But hey at least that deli is out of your life. One thing about the health club? You never have to worry about tongue."

The Babecat gave me this smile and went to this other room in our apt where we have the TV. I didn't want her to feel guilty or anything, but pretty much all I could think about for the rest of the night was tongue.

And not just deli tongue.

THE MUMBLY LIPS
by Nefertiti Snorkjutt—*November 14*

I have been in something of a, well, *pother* ever since the presidential election was lost by Reformed Misogyny candidate Slappy Goering, a former comedian who is also deep.

I was in this pother all weekend, and I believe I, well, I'm almost *certain* I kicked every piece of furniture in my house, including some custom pieces with straps on the arms. By the time I was, well, the next thing I knew I was *famished* and ended up eating a half dozen rolls in a local bakery, where the employees call me "mami" and where I once had to break a man's hand with my buttocks.

And I am, well, *sleepless* at the thought that a genius like Slappy Goering is at the nightly disposal of his well, *wife*—a blonde *twit* who gives no evidence that she understands a man's constant need for discipline. What, I have been wondering, is my social duty in a situation like, well, *this one*?

Then my agent—Allison Muffplug—called to remind me that I owe her a script for *Perp & Vic: Men Are Bastards Unit*, and I was rescued! Yes, *rescued*, for in writing that script I found myself on a healing journey.

Perp & Vic is the most successful cop show ever broadcast. *Perp & Vic: Men Are Bastards Unit* is one of its spin-offs, and I have been writing scripts for that, well, *program* for the

last, oh, I don't know, *year?* At all events, it is about a squad that investigates reports of criminal misogyny. The characters are Detective Parkdrive, a square-jawed woman with an uncertain hairstyle, and her male partner, a reformed misogynist named Redhook.
Here is some of the script I turned in.

Parkdrive is behind the steering wheel of a luxurious squad car. Beside her, in the passenger seat, is Redhook.

Parkdrive: I don't feel good about this one, Redhook. I usually look forward to kicking misogynist butt.

Redhook: I hear you, Parkdrive. Usually it isn't the man dropping the dime on the woman.

Parkdrive: And such a good-looking man. Did you vote for him, Redhook?

Redhook: Nipsy Himmler? Sure. I thought everyone did. The great thing about him is he makes you laugh *and* makes you think. When I think of what this country could be with a Himmler at the helm...

Parkdrive: Yeah. Tell me about it.

The car stops in front of a mansion with lots of upstairs rooms that could easily be soundproofed, if only the right woman had a free hand.

Parkdrive and Redhook step out of the car and walk to the front door. Parkdrive rings the bell.

Parkdrive: This better not be some male trick to frame an innocent woman, Redhook. I mean, my first female misogynist!

Redhook: Easy, Parkdrive. Maybe it's a mistake. This Nipsy Himmler, sure, he seems like a genius, maybe even a messiah, but he's not a professional. He could be wrong about his wife. Don't get so worked up.

An incredibly handsome man answers the door. He is ashen with fright.

Parkdrive: Congressman Himmler? I'm Detective Parkdrive. This is my partner, Detective Redhook.

Himmler(dreamily): Your jaw…it's…so square…

Parkdrive: Thank you.

Redhook: Enough jaw talk. Why don't you tell us why you phoned, Congressman?

Himmler: I…was about to do the mumbly lips on my wife tonight when I noticed something that, well, I just can't overlook anymore.

Redhook: And that's what, Congressman?

Himmler: I…well, I…

Parkdrive: Let me try to walk you through it, Congressman. At first she wouldn't let you, right? She told you that she, like all women, had internalized sexual stigmas, and that if she let you do the mumbly lips you would have to understand that it would force her to confront her doubts about her viability as a sexual entity, and that when it was over you would owe her a big favor. Isn't that right?

Himmler: No. Not even close. In fact, she begged me for it.

Redhook: Uh-oh...

Parkdrive: Bitch! Where is she?!

Redhook: Easy, Parkdrive.

Himmler: In the living room. Follow me.

Parkdrive and Redhook follow Himmler into the living room. Seated on the sofa is an obvious slut in a pink slip.

Himmler: I'm a failed novelist. She wears that to taunt me.

Himmler lights a cigarette with an oversized lighter as Parkdrive and Redhook approach the slut.

Parkdrive: Please don't stand up. I'm Detective Parkdrive. This is my partner, Detective Redhook.

Slut: You know you have these really huge jawbones?

Parkdrive: I hear you got some oral sex tonight.

Slut: Mmm. Mumbly lips from a Stephen King wannabe.

Parkdrive: Mind if I ask you some questions?

Slut: Go right ahead.

Parkdrive: Why do you have sex? Is it for fun or for empowerment?

Slut: Um…fun?

Redhook: Bad guess, hot stuff.

The slut just giggles. Parkdrive unholsters her pistol and shoots the slut in the face. Brains and blood splatter the wall behind her.

Redhook: Well, if anyone had it coming, she did.

Parkdrive holsters her gun. She is visibly shaken. Redhook holds her.

Parkdrive: I can't believe I did that…

Redhook: Keep it steady, Parkdrive. Remember, you're the victim here. It can't be easy, seeing your first female misogynist. Nobody could internalize that.

Himmler: I…I don't know how to thank you.

He blows a smoke ring.

Parkdrive: Yes, you do.

All right, I admit I was a little, well, angry when I wrote that scene. Still, I didn't expect that, well, the day after I faxed it to Allison she would call me back and say that the producers of the show thought it contained too much "woman-on-woman violence."

"But…but…did they see what *kind* of woman?!"

"I know, dear," Allison said. "I'm just telling you what they said, and I'm afraid it's final."

"Well, Allison," I said, "I don't know who these 'producers' are, but I smell a scrotum."

"Nef, dear," she said with a sigh, "I'm smelling it all day long."

SKIDMORES
by Barry Fest—*November 19*

Well, my friends, busy weeks at the Belverton University Press. Yes, busy weeks. The holidays always bring on a rush to get out the seasonal materials, but I think we have everything out the door at last. My own contribution to the lot is a monograph entitled *The Myth of the Gifted Child*, which was not going to qualify as a holiday publication until my new companion—Mickey Snaketail—thought to have the graphics department put a little bow on the word "Gifted."

Once the rush settled down, I decided again to try to confront Moliere about the tongue-exerciser she had given me several weeks earlier.

Mickey, who was hired by my wife—Dr. Wharton-Stone—to chaperone me and keep me safe from the supposed wiles of the gothic Moliere, was seated at the side of my desk when I summoned her. He smiled an affable smile, attired as usual in his beige, elbow-patched sports jacket and his crumpled, black-and-yellow tie. When Moliere walked in he made a note in his memo pad.

Moliere smiled at Mickey and flung herself into the chair across the desk from me. She was wearing a black t-shirt over her massive dragon tattoo. The t-shirt had white lettering across the front that spelled out the words THANK GOD IT'S HUMP DAY.

"Moliere," I began cautiously, "I need to speak to you about the...tongue exerciser."

"Yeah?" she asked, her eyes brightening. "How're the exercises goin'? Toughenin' up that tongue, I hope!"

"Let's talk about that some other time," I said. I turned to my chaperone. "Could you excuse us, Mickey?" I asked.

Mickey shrugged, smiled, and kept writing in his pad. I sighed.

"Hey, Snake-boy," Moliere said, "how 'bout gettin' a couple venti drips for me and the boss?"

Mickey's eyes widened. He hopped to his feet and went out the door.

Moliere giggled. "He really is obedient," she said. "But ya kinda have to have the rack for it." She stood up and came around my desk, raising the distinctive tingle in my corduroys as I saw the long, tulle skirt advancing.

She sat on my desk in front of me. I inhaled, not too obviously, I think, and took in her intoxicating, female musk. I cleared my throat, took the tongue-exerciser out of my desk drawer, and placed it in her lap.

"Moliere, were you aware that your tongue-exerciser looks precisely like a, well...a *ball-gag?*"

"A what gag?"

"A *ball*-gag," I said, "is a nefarious accessory of sadomasochistic role-play. Or so I hear from Dr. Wharton-Stone."

"Brass *knockers!*" she exclaimed. "Well, Dr. Worthinghammer should know!"

"I think *you* should know that the night you sent me home with that...that—"

"Tongue-exerciser."

"Yes. Well, the night you sent me home with it was the first of three nights that I spent with Dr. Wharton-Stone's leg strapped across my chest."

She smiled a smile which, on a middle-aged man, could have been described only as *lascivious*.

"Fuh-*reaky*," she said. "But why would she do that? I mean, if she's into something fellatical you can definitely talk to me about it."

"Fellatical? Is that a real word?"

"It was in my dorm!—So why did Dr. Skank pin you like that?"

"Moliere, if you must know, Dr. Sk—that is, *Wharton-Stone* pinned me down because she thought that, unrestrained, I might go out looking for you."

In what must have been a maternal reflex, Moliere seized me by the back of my head, no doubt to clutch me to her bosom. But the angle at which we sat meant my head reached only as far as her lap. She held me there, pinned against the tongue-exerciser.

"Oh, poor boss!" she said with a pitying chuckle. "Now why would she think you would go lookin' for *me*, hmmmmm?"

"Well, that was unwarranted speculation on her part," I said into her skirt. "Please let me up, Moliere."

She released my head. My face itched from the tulle.

"Did you get up?" she asked as I rubbed my nose.

"Huh?"

"When she nodded off. Did you get up?"

"I couldn't. Her grip was too tight."

"Even while she was sleeping?"

"Yes," I admitted. "I am not proud of it."

"Weak abs, huh?"

"Yes. *Very* weak."

"Well…" she said, her eyes wandering to some point distant. "Don't you think you should do somethin' about that?"

"What do you have in mind? Sit-ups?"

She thought for a moment, and then her eyes widened in the manner of a ten year-old who has just seen her name on the big package under the Christmas tree.

"Skidmores!" she shouted.

"Skidmores? What is a skidmore?"

"I'll show ya! Lie down on your back on the floor!"

"Moliere, it is…a working day, after all."

"We won't do a whole routine," she insisted. "I'll just show you, and then you can do them in your spare time. You *will* need a partner, though."

"Well, all right," I whined as I got out of the chair and lay on the rug. Hm. A fuzzy, Styrofoam peanut lay just out of reach under my bottom desk drawer.

As I tried to recall the provenance of said peanut, Moliere stood above me and hiked her skirt up to about her knees. From my vantage point I could see her nude legs disappearing into shadow just before they met. She lay beside me and put one of said legs across my neck.

"Is this where she put it?" she asked.

"Lower. Across my chest."

She moved her leg down until it transversed my sternum. "Now try sittin' up!" she said.

I tried, but to no avail. Damned women and their iron thighs!

"I'll make it lighter and we'll work our way up bit by bit," she said. "Don't worry, boss. Before you know it, I'll be sitting on your chest and straddling your collarbone. *That's* a skidmore!"

"I'm not so sure you should do that, Moliere," I said. "I'll smother under all this tulle."

"Don't worry, boss. I can hike it up *lots* further."

At that moment Mickey Snaketail entered my field of vision. He stood just above Moliere with a large cup of coffee in each fist. His eyes were wide with alarm as they darted back and forth between us. Moliere saw my eyes go to him, a little apprehensively I should think, then she smiled.

"Grab his feet, Snake-boy," she commanded when she saw him.

He put the coffee down on the desktop and took me by my ankles. Then he released them, jotted something down in his memo pad, and took hold of them again.

Moliere looked at me and giggled. "Least he didn't take a picture!" she said.

PERSONALITY CRISIS
by Desmond Cork—*November 25*

Okay like last time? I wanted to answer this Indian guy about why teenage girls high on their first jolt of estro make love-slaves out of male rockers and this cat named Woody Allen but I didn't get a chance because the Babecat had this thing where she got fired from her deli job over some tongue and she needed somebody to nod and say "whoa" now and then.

And like today I'm checking out the ol' inbox and I see this email which I think has a pretty worthy question because it shows the confusion people have about the New York rock scene.

> Hey, Mr. Cork,
>
> I'm writin this because I guess you could say I'm a concerned parent. I walked into my bedroom late yesterday afternoon and I found my son Kris posed in front of the window. It was freakin weird. At first I didn't know it was him. He was just this shadow against the pale white light comin from the window. But then he flicked on the bedroom lights in this kind of dramatic...well, *flick*—and I could

see he was wearin these high-heeled boots, a bouffant wig, and lipstick smeared across his lips. (He has plump lips like Mick.)

I'm ganderin at this freakin sight and then he says, "Hi, *Dad*. I found your *stuff* under your *bed*."

And I just said to myself: "Uh-oh." Cuz the stuff he was talkin about was my mint vinyl copy of the New York Dolls' *Too Much Too Soon*, and my New York Dolls gear, which he was wearin.

So he told me that he was rummagin around down there lookin for porn. Imagine his shock when he found *my* stash. I was tryin to tell him what the Dolls can mean to a guy when he ran out of the room with tears streakin the red stuff on his cheeks. I heard the front door slam and then his voice outside as he ran down the street screamin, "My Dad loves pansies! My Dad loves pansies!"

Do you think you can help me with this, Mr. Cork? What can I tell my kid about the New York Dolls?

Like I said,
A Concerned Parent

(Whoa. I think when I was a kid the only thing my old man had under his bed was a t-shirt that said "YABA-DABA-DOO!" and a poster of Fred doing Wilma Dino-style.)

Well, the first thing this concerned parent cat has to tell his kid is that the New York Dolls were *not* pansies. They had to dress up like babes in self-defense.

See, the Dolls learned their lesson from what happened to the original original Ramones, yeah? Like, they learned that to be totally safe from the estro that makes chicks animals you pretty much have to disguise yourself as—

Just as I'm writing that cats the Babecat's phone goes off only the Babecat went out to make treat purchases for her kitty (oh yeah we have a cat, cats) and forgot to take her phone with her.

So I pick up and say, "Yoo-hoo?"

And this dude's voice says kind of nervous: "Is um Lola there?"

And I say: "Nice dialing, dude," and I flip down. But what's weird? The Babecat has caller ID on her phone and when this dude called the ID said "Bruce," which I figured must be her code name for wrong numbers.

I'm about to get back to the ol' Concerned Parent when rrrrrrring!—the phone again!

I flip up and I can like hear this cat breathing. I'm a little fried, yeah? "Hey. Dude. No. Lola. Caprice?"—And I like flip down.

"Oh my God!" I hear from behind me and cats, I jumped about a foot off my chair. I turn around and it's the Babecat.

"Des. Dude. Was that call for me, dude?"

"Nope. It was some cat calling for this Lola babe."

And the Babecat slides down into that deep sofa I like to nap on and says, "Des. Dude. My name is Lola, dude!"

I'm like wait a minute.

So she gives me the kind of look that used to wake me up screaming for my mommy. You know where the eyes get so wide you think they're going to leak off the edges of the face and the mouth gets zigzag crazy.

Then she just kind of smiles and says, "It's okay Des. Don't worry about it."

I kind of chuckle and stare at her because in my nightmare? That's what the zigzag lady says before she bites me off at the neck.

Then she says: "I'll call them back later. Did…did they say who they were?"

"Nope," I say sort of breezy since I'm pretty sure it's not the nightmare now, "but the ol' caller ID said 'Bruce.'"

There's this kind of pause and the Babecat is looking at me like I just sprung a pop quiz on her or something and then she says, "Des. Remember the cat who fired me on my cell a few weeks ago? That was Bruce."

And I'm like: "Whoa. Babecat. Way not to burn bridges!"

She just kept sort of smiling and I thought I saw her eyes get a little watery. Then she came over and stroked my hair the way I did to my dog Buster when I was twelve and we knew it was his last trip to the vet.

So the Babecat goes out, right? And like I'm trying to concentrate on telling this cat why the New York Dolls weren't pansies but this Bruce jive keeps bugging me. And I'm remembering the night Bruce fired the Babecat from her deli job. It took him like twenty minutes? And at the end she was squealing these little gulpy squeals. And…and it was like one o'clock in the morning, cats. I mean if you're firing somebody that's *way* late.

So I squint my eyes at the wall real steely-like cause I'm beginning to think the Babecat isn't giving me the whole deal on this one. Was she still working at the deli? And this Bruce…

I mean the Babecat might not know it but a cat can tell when some dude is putting starter moves on his babe.

A NEW G-SPOT
by Nefertiti Snorkjutt—*November 29*

So I'm enduring—well, perhaps not *enduring*, but certainly *spending*—far more time in the basement gym. With barbells and dumbbells and benches and flies. You can see my lat definition straight through the vinyl!

For the occasional laugh I have posted a picture of Slappy Goering's wife—Cindy "Horseface" Goering—on my electronic dartboard. Usually I am disdainful—well, perhaps *disapproving* is more apt—of electronic gadgets. But this dartboard lets you program it to make sounds, and whenever I hit Mrs. Goering in the eyeball it sobs for eight seconds.

But it hasn't been what you might call a *smooth* campaign. It has been, well, *interrupted* with demands for rewrites of my latest television script, in which Detective Parkdrive empowered herself by blowing out the brains of a slut.

In my second draft I had Detective Parkdrive "harvest" the slut with a farm combine. But that too was considered "too violent." So then I had the slut gang-frenched by a troop of Boy Scouts with strep. The testicle-toting producers of the show said her death in that ver—well, *revision* was "too slow and agonizing."

My last rewrite had the slut bitten in half by an alligator. I think you might, well, find it *odd*, but the most empowering moment of writing that script came when I had to spell out the slut's last scream. To wit, "AIEEEEEEEEE-AH-AH-NO-OHMYGOD-AIEEEEEEEEEE!!!!!"

The producers feared reprisals from family-values advocates and would not agree to accept this ending until I changed the OHMYGOD part of the scream to OHMY-GOSH, which I finally did at the urging of my agent, Allison Muffplug.

With the script out of the, well, *way*, I hung on the wall by the dartboard a map of the Goering mansion and grounds. It is a large, white map with squiggly blue lines for roads and black triangles, or, rather, *pyramids* for bushes, hm?

You see, Slappy's mansion is on a hill covered with shrubs and little trees. The money he got as a comedian means he can employ an army of gardeners. And all of these gardeners are Japanese except for one, who happens to be a deaf Italian of some gentility, with a graying pencil mustache and a green ascot, who smokes short, brown cigarettes and starts many of his sentences with the phrase, "I will tell you about women…"

I have, well, *marked* the location of the Italian with a magnet in the shape of an anchovy. I have also marked—with a little pink pony—the place in the Goering driveway where Horseface emerges daily from her SUV after running her little wifey errands.

And I have marked my stakeout position at the bottom of the hill, near the Italian, with a little black whip.

Pony at the top, anchovy in the middle, whip at the bottom…I was ready to, well, *move*.

My plan was to surprise the, um, well, the horse-faced hag by leaping out of the shrubbery in a black rubber cat suit and scaring her into the next town with low growls. Once she understood that Slappy was *my* property, I would let her settle the more mundane separation matters with him over the telephone.

So I drove out to the Goering mansion one afternoon a few days ago and parked at the foot of the hill. I was, well, *off*, you might say, on the side of the dirt road that led to the mansion, waiting for the deaf gardener to wander off and prune something. But it seems that in late November most plants are dead, so he sat on his little stool in a green and white parka and whittled with a knife so long he could have used it to lift my skirt.

I stared at him through the binoculars. "Move, *amico mio*," I muttered under my breath. "*Andiamo*, eh?"

It looked like it might be a long wait while he whittled, so I took out my tape recorder and began making voice notes for my next teleplay. "Parkdrive and Redhook bust an Italian pimp..." I brainstormed into the microphone.

Then I noticed something peculiar. On the hill above the gardener's head I could see the Goering driveway, and it, well, it *looked* as if the—what is it called?—*SUV* was already there, parked! Was Horseface home? Was she already in the house? Had I missed my chance?

I jumped out of my car to get a better look. As I was hoisting the binoculars I heard a snotty little receptionist voice from a position to my rear.

"Looking for something, Rubberjugs?" it asked.

I turned and saw Horseface leaning against a nearby elm tree, her legs crossed at the ankles and her hands jammed into the pockets of a red fleece vest.

She sounded rather, well, *peculiar*. As if a brain were operating her mouth.

"I made you days ago, casing the place," she said. "You see the monitor?" She pointed to a six-gun shaped, white camera on top of a thin rail. "We put it there a few weeks back to see if we could catch the Italian gardener bandersnatching the Jamaican Webmaster from Slappy.com."

"*Al*, well, *fresco*?"

"Yes," she said. "Webmasters have disgusting kinks."

Remembering my original scheme—that is, my original *plan*—I jumped a few paces toward her and growled very low. She didn't move.

"Trying to scare me?" she asked. Then she smiled at me, yes, she smiled at me with...I dread writing it...*condescension*. "You have me confused with the bimbo I was forced to play on the campaign trail. Americans don't like a candidate with a wife that thinks, so I dumbed it so far down the only people who would talk to me were part-time Santas."

So I balled up my fist and I took a—well, I *swung* at her. She sidestepped, took me by the arm, and pulled me off balance. I fell in the bushes. She jumped on top of me, smothering me in fleece. Somehow, I got the fingers of one hand entwined in her hair, and she got one hand around my ear.

With our free hands we slapped each other to a standstill.

She struggled up and fell against the hood of my car, panting. "I know you want Slappy," she said, "but I've invested too much time in training that idiot. When I met him he had no idea how to find a woman's G-spot. It took me a year, but now he can track one down blindfolded from across a hotel room."

I was sitting in the dirt, but I tried to sound haughty anyway. "It took you a, well, *year?*" I sneered.

"Oh yes. And I'd have taken two, if necessary." She straightened up. "The former-comedian money is *that good.*"

And without so much as a good-bye, she turned on her heel and strutted up the road to the mansion. I walked back to my car, plotting my next, well, what you might call *gambit*.

Then I noticed, on the front seat, the tape recorder I had been dictating into. It was still recording. I rewound until I found it, faint, but enough to recognize the voice.

"I've invested too much time in training that idiot," it said. "Too much time in training that idiot...that idiot... idiot...idiot..."

I looked up the hill past the deaf gardener, who was still whittling away, oblivious to the struggle—well, perhaps not struggle, but at least *wrangle*—that had just taken place.

"Well, *sister*," I said under my breath, "looks to me like there's a new G-spot in the hotel room."

HORNY GOAT WEED
by Barry Fest—*December 4*

 Friends, please permit me an admittedly presumptuous question:
 Have you ever had a tattooed girl strap her nude leg across your chest, pinning you to the floor, solely to provide you the resistance necessary to improve your abdominal muscles?
 I imagine your answer is *nay*. Well, I have had such a woman do just that for me. Repeatedly. Day after day.
 You may be shocked. You may wish to shake me by my fifty-percent cashmere lapels and say, "Fest, why not simply use a long bar with weights on each end for resistance? Or one of those machines with the giant rubber bands? Why go to the lengths, the inconvenience, the *trouble* of having a tattooed girl in a long tulle dress and dragon tattoo pin you down with a leg like a deadbolt across your chest, forcing you to pry her thighs apart as you struggle to sit?"
 I cede the point, my friends. But the weights and the rubber bands do not come with the sweet musk of Moliere, and that is my addiction.
 Since Moliere has begun assisting me in this manner, I have become a veritable dynamo at crunching upward as she clenches down. So well have I done, in fact, that I have no

trouble escaping the flannel-swathed legs of my wife—Dr. Wharton-Stone—which she is wont to lay across me as she sleeps.

In our last session, on the floor of my office, Moliere was so taken with my improved condition that at one point she reached over, stroked my hair, and said, I believe rather soulfully, "Boss, you're gonna take your first skidmore any day now."

"And a skidmore is where you sit facing me on my chest..."

"With my skirt hiked up way high so you don't smother in the tulle."

"And that is really going to help develop my abdominals?" I asked, trying not to sound too skeptical.

"Oh," she said, looking deeply into my eyes again, "it'll be *great.*"

Lest you think she is using these exercise sessions simply to get out of her work duties, allow me the opportunity to relate a further instance of her maternal interest.

Last week I began to manifest symptoms of a cold. On such occasions I generally resign myself to suffering through four days of misery as the cold runs its course, but Moliere would have none of that. She sent me immediately to the herbalist with a list of natural remedies she insisted would speed my recovery.

So I hied myself to the medicine man with Mickey Snake-tail in tow.

I showed Mickey the list, and he signaled—silently as always—the twenty-something clerk, who was at that moment standing on a metal stepladder replacing one of the garish bulbs above a light-diffusing panel in the ceiling. He climbed down, an inscrutable smirk—common among members of the mercantile class—upon his face. He wore a little white shirt, black tie, and his hair, well, his hair was that of a film noir gangster: glistening, ebony, curly, deep.

"What up, fellas?" the lad asked. Mickey handed him the list.

"Hmm," the fellow said. "Horny goat weed. Well, well... flag's flyin' at half mast, is it?"

I tried for a half-second to decipher the question, then gave up. "It's for my cold," I explained hoarsely.

"Sure it is," the clerk said, winking. "Staff sergeant's callin' in sick, is he? Well, don't worry, chief, the doctor is in."

My throat was too sore for oral remonstrations, so I let his familiarity go with a stern look. The clerk led Mickey and me down a sterile aisle and stopped in front of a stack of mahogany shelves. The gaudy sign above the aisle featured a semi-nude man in shorts and a blond woman with a broad grin—relieved, no doubt, that her boyfriend was recovering from his cold.

The clerk snatched up two bottles and handed them to me.

"The labels on the bottles say what this stuff is good for," he said.

"Colds?" I asked.

"Yeah," he said, again with an impudent wink. "Colds, the flu, faintin' spells. Expecially faintin' spells."

Then immediately he lost his smile, grasped my arm with doctoral authority, and looked into my eyes. "But I hafta warn ya, chief: the FDA has not evaluated these statements."

That sent shivers down my spine, shivers that were quickly replaced by a round of perspiration. I looked at Mickey. There was no hint of his usual affability. He was doleful, drawn, nay, *haggard*.

He swallowed hard, then jotted something down on his memo pad. When he finished he turned it to me.

THE FDA MIGHT NOT KNOW EVERYTHING

it said.

I slapped him hard across the mouth.

"Don't you ever write that again!" I shrieked, wincing at the throat pain. A woman in a fur coat looked at us from an island of mechanical foot massagers and rolled her eyes.

Mickey capped his pen, grinned once furtively, and hung his head.

FOR THE CHILDREN
by Nefertiti Snorkjutt—*December 10*

I have the goods on Cindy Goering. Mmm. Perhaps not the *goods*, but at least the *lowdown*. It is a *tape*-recording of Mrs. Horseface Goering saying that Slappy is an idiot and, well, so much more.

The night after our little encounter I got out the tape player and called Horseface on the telephone. I announced who I was and she chuckled a little. "Want to talk to the Slapster? He's working right now, if you know what I mean."

"I really *don't* know what you mean," I said. "I called to speak to *you*." That's when I played her this recording of her own voice:

> I know you want Slappy, but I've invested too much time in training that idiot. When I met him he had no idea how to find a woman's G-spot. It took me a year, but now he can track one down blindfolded from across a hotel room.

I clicked, hm, I guess I mean I *turned* off the tape and heard the bitch laughing.

"Tell you what, Horseface," I said, "if you want to keep your share of the former-comedian money, take those little girly pink things you like to wear and move out now and, um, Slappy never has to hear that tape."

"Oooooo," she said when she caught her breath. "Can I have a day to cry about it, Leatherslats?"

Before I could tell her no, she turned away from the phone and said, "Take a break, Slap. You know the cougar with the rubber cushion? She has something she wants to say to you."

A second later, Slappy was on the phone.

"Snorkety!" he said. "Nyuk! Nyuk! Nyuk!—Hold on, I have to blow my nose."

Well, I was, I suppose you would have to say *flabbergasted*, but I played him the tape and…he laughed!

"Yep, hate to admit it," he said. "But I was kind of a loser! Nyuk! Nyuk! Nyuk! Sometimes Cindy has to help me out, even now. Wearing a crotchless body stocking and sitting in a low chair seems to do the trick, though."

"I…um…well, I…*well!*" I said.

"Say, Snorkety," he went on, "didja hear? The Goering Campaign is pushing for a recount!"

"Of the, um, *vote?*" I asked.

"Natch," he said. "The whole recount effort is being spearheaded by the Children for Goering Committee. Isn't that sweet? Children! Nyuk! Nyuk! Nyuk! For Goering!"

"Hmm," I said. "Children…but, well, I mean, why children? Can't the really tall politicians step right over them?"

He seemed, well he *was*, I think, *hurt*.

"Well, Snorkety…" he whined, "everyone knows the children wanted Slappy to be president. But who did their parents vote for? The Republican. Ick. The other one. Blech. Now here's what I've got on the noodle, Snorks. I'm already happily married, so I can't fulfill your manster needs, but how about coming to work on the recount project, hmm?"

"But, well, Slappy," I said, in something of a…I guess I will have to admit it was a *come-hither* tone, "what's in it for the cougar with the rubber cushion?"

He sounded hurt again.

"Snorkety, please," he said. "Do it for the *children*."

My first task on the, well, on the *task* force. Hm. Well, my first task was to hire some private investigators to search high and low throughout the American—well, *America* to find evidence of a conspiracy to deprive Slappy of his presidency and the children of their Slappy.

My second, oh, *chore* was to organize a children's rally demanding that the US Senate conduct an investigation into anti-Slappy intimidation at polling booths nationwide. The keynote speaker at the rally was a fat little girl with a runny nose who won a contest for who could write the best protest poem on behalf of Slappy. It was, well, the *title* of it was "They Stoled My Slappy From Me," and it went like this. (Readers with what I think—well, *sensitive* readers might want to be forewarned: both her parents are high school gym teachers.)

> *They stoled my Slappy from me*
> *They stoled him sure as shit*
> *While he was out campaigning*
> *The wringer had his tit.*
>
> *My folks both voted for him*
> *They said his balls were brass*
> *But someone stoled my Slappy*
> *Democracy my ass*

She's twelve.

After that recital, I well, I *sidled* up to Slappy. Thinking that we were alone, I reached over to stroke his face with the handle of my riding crop.

"Don't touch my Slappy!" shouted the runny-nosed little poetess. She stepped out of, well, *I* didn't see her, that's for sure, and she stood between we two grown-ups and folded her arms across her chest.

"Hmm," I said. I thumb—yes, *thumbed* my riding crop. Absentmindedly.

"Yes, please stop," Slappy said gently, looking into my eyes and moving my crop away from his face. "Stop...for the children."

I looked at the vulgar gym brat. "Wipe your nose," I said.

That very...yes, *very* night the private investigators I had hired to look into the fifty-state anti-Slappy conspiracy reported back. They didn't have much on the infernal cabal (as the one with the ivory-handled revolver called it), but they did have an audiotape recording. A recording of Horseface. Here's what she was saying *this* time.

> All right, boys. I'm doing my part to keep this pinhead from winning anything. Who do you think told him it was a good idea to promise not to get an erection until after Election Day? Was that a stroke of genius or what? That promise was so stupid he will never be elected to anything again, not even roastmaster. Now whose (bleep) do I have to (bleep) to get an invite to the Clinton Inauguration?

"Who added the bleeps?" I, well, *demanded*.

"I did!" shouted the one with the ivory-handled pistols. "I heard there was kids involved!"

Well, I took that tape straight to Slappy, and he kicked the little bitch out of his study, well, I think they used to say *forthwith*. "And take your little girly pink things with you!" he shouted as she swiveled down the walk to the driveway. She turned, gave us the finger, got in her SUV, and tore away.

Once she was gone, Slappy paced his study, nyukking absently. He sat at his desk and cradled his head in his hands. I went to a...*position*—or perhaps *station*—behind him and began to massage his shoulders. I had something in my purse for him, but I thought I would give him some time to heal first.

He lifted his head out of his hands for a moment but did not turn to look at me. "Nef, did you notice...I don't know if this is from living with her all that time, but...did you notice that she has a face just like a horse? Swear to God, waking up with her next to me sometimes, it was just like that scene with the movie producer in *The Godfather*. I couldn't call her 'pal-o-mine' because I was afraid I'd slip and say 'palomino.' I—"

"Enough," I said, "with the *gags*."

He turned to me. He was looking—oh...His eyes were *urgent*.

"Nef," he said. "You can't tell anyone about how Cindy betrayed me. I mean, what will the children think? My own wife sold us out. How will that make them feel? Would they ever be able to trust another decision of mine? You can't tell 'em, Nef! Promise you won't tell 'em!"

That was enough time for healing, I thought. I went to my purse and took out a choker and tossed it in front of him on his desk. I could see the...yes, I could...I could see the brass spikes reflected in his eyes.

"It...it looks like a dog collar," he said.

"Put it on, Slappy," I said.

"But...why, Nef?"

"Do it," I said, "for the *children*."

FISHNETS AND GARTERS
by Desmond Cork—*December 14*

Hey cats. So I never got around to answering the ol' Concerned Parent about the New York Dolls last time. And like you cats keep sending the question nasties and I keep trying to answer but I'm having a hard time porting it all off lately.

Like casing point? I just got this email from some babe named Janstasia in New South Wales, Australia, and it's really begging for a shout back.

> Hey scholar man. I heard this Livvy Tyler the actress or act<u>or</u> or whatever was raised thinking she was the daughter of Toddy Rundgren but she was in reality life the daughter of Stevey Tyler from the band Aerosmith. This is weird because she should have just known from her last name being Tyler that something was up at least that's what I'm thinking.
>
> But I really like Livvy Tyler the actress or act<u>or</u> and not only that but I was also raised like her thinking Toddy Rundgren was in reality my dad!

See the tubbyguts who called himself my dad was this payola solicitor for radio 3BO in Sydney and he was <u>really</u> sloppy and he factually weighed like 9000 lbs. not very tasty for my mom!

(And he always had this dried-up egg yoke on the corner of his lip when he freddied out for work in the AM. —<u>Ewwww</u>!)

My mom would see me looking at him like I was factually going to puke and as soon as he turned his back she would touch me on the hand and whisper "Don't worry about him luv your real dad is Toddy Rundgren."

That made me feel a <u>lot</u> better scholar man! So I got into the whole rocking scene and when I was sixteen I started wearing fishnets and garters instead of pantyhose. That was when boys started sleeping over in my room and my oil whale faker of a so-called dad would come in in the morning in his baggy underpants and shiny shoes and kick them and call them pischers in a totally high voice and I would shout at him "Jam it shammer!"

The boys were scared of him but my mom and me just laughed till he ran off weeping he was so fat and jiggly!

Do you think that makes Livvy Tyler and me soul mates?

Yours very truly ;-)
Stasia

Okay like I guess it's possible that down in Sydney they don't know this but there are a *lot* of chicks who were raised thinking Todd Rundgren was their old man. Like in L.A.? Every strip—

So cats I'm writing that down and out pops the Babecat from the bedroom and she's dressed just like this Janstasia babe dressed when she was sixteen, yeah? In fishnets and garters. So I'm like, "Hey Babecat, no pantyhose?"

She wrinkled her nose at me and picked up her purse.

"So Babecat," I bold on, "where to this eve?"

And she says, "Decorating the deli," really quick, which is a little off to the bogus side for me because she used to pause real long when I asked her about where she was going.

"So they really changed the deli into a veggie deli, huh?"

"Yep."

"So they have—"

"Tofu turkey slices, tofu tongue, tofu ham, veggie burgers...they're thinking of changing the name to Yo Soy."

"Cool," I said, but I'm thinking why is the Babecat telling me all this stuff? And why so fast? It's getting tray suspicious, cats.

"And like Bruce is going to be there?" I asked.

"Oh yeah," she said. "He's the *boss*."

And she split.

There was something about the way she said "boss" that I was not down with, cats. And just like last time I was pretty sure I wasn't getting the whole story.

So I thought about it for a while. Then I sat in this other chair and thought about it. Then I got up and flung on my street clothes which is like a belt and started out the door. Then this voice in my head says real soft-like, "Des. Dude. Where you off to, dude?" And it hits me: I don't know where this Bruce cat lives. And I don't know how to track dudes down and make them back off when I nail them. I don't know any of that stuff.

The door was open and I was in the middle of the doorway staring out real steely-like and thinking and Mrs. Liang my next door neighbor walks into her apartment with these big shopping bags and as she goes past she gives me this little smile like she sees me standing in my doorway *every* night.

"Is...Babecat home?" she asks real polite-like.

"Nope, Mrs. Liang," I say, "the Babecat is out. But I'm gonna get her back."

She giggles. "Well you come by some night she not here. Mr. Liang, he in Hong Kong next six week."

"Well, okay Mrs. Liang," I say. "But I'm not so hot at fixing stuff."

So she giggles again. "You come by," she says and dodges into her apt.

I got all steely again. "Now what I need," I'm saying out loud to help me concentrate (which was tough cats, because this Mrs. Liang? She's short but she has this happening rack), "is somebody who's tough. Somebody with experience making cats yelp and plead."

And luckily? I know somebody just like that. So I went back into my apartment and closed my door and snapped up my cell.

"Yellooooooo!" says this dude's voice on the other end.

"Hey," I said, "is this Nef Snorkjutt's phone?"

"For a million dollars, the answer iiiiiiiiiiiis...YES!" shouted this weird cat. "Nyuk! Nyuk! Nyuk!"

"Whoa! Is this like Slappy Goering? I think I voted for you, dude!"

But this nyukking cat never answers. I hear a rip and a scrape and a high squeegy and then a few hard slaps.

In the distance I can hear: "Ow! Nyuk! Ow! Nyuk!"

Then Nef comes on and I like say my name and stuff.

"Desmond, well, I'm, I guess you could say I'm *surprised* to hear from you," she says. "Hm. Perhaps not *surprised*, but at least *taken aback*. I thought you were, well, *afraid* of me."

Then she laughs this cackling laugh like she does before she shows you the rope in her purse.

So I told her how I needed her to help me find this deli-owning cat who I think is trying to flash nasty with my babe. I think I heard her yawn a couple times and then laugh when a dog barked in the background.

Then I told her how the cat's name was Bruce and how the Babecat's real name was Lola.

I thought I heard her breathe in really fast. "Shut up!" she shouted at her dog.

It stopped barking and said, "Ssssssorry!"

"Did you—now, Des, very, let us say, *slowly*. Did you say her name is *Lola?* And his name is *Bruce?*"

"Yup," I said.

"All, well, *right*. I'll tell you what you do there, my skinny young co-work—well, *colleague*. I want you to put on your belt. Then I want you to meet me in half an hour in front of the offices of the university press."

"Whoa. Nef...you're gonna help me find 'em?"

"That's right," she said. "We're going to find that, well, that *couple*, and they are going back to what I think you might call *obedience* school."

"Nyuk! Nyuk! Nyuk!" said this voice in the background. And cats, I'm pretty sure I voted for that dude.

THE LEGEND OF MOO RIDLEY
by Barry Fest—*December 19*

Yesterday I was at a family reunion of sorts. Every December my wife—Dr. Wharton-Stone—calls together a convocation of psychologists and psychiatrists (all blood relations of hers and in-laws of mine) for a no-holds-barred analysis of the foregoing year. This retrospective usually devolves into a review of the progress I am making with my personality, the current version of which I formally adopted on New Year's Day 2000 after a marathon viewing of the old television series, *The Saint*.

My goal was to become suave.

There are two schools of thought on my personality. (Dr. Wharton-Stone's extended family of Stones and Whartons is large, vast, nay, *huge*, and can support easily two schools of thought, each with its own peer review.) The first school of thought maintains that I am on the wrong footing and should adopt a new personality forthwith; the second school regards my current personality as sufficient, but last year recommended that I acquire some marketing skills to get said personality "out there."

These end-of-year sessions tend to be as humiliating as they are fascinating, and my only respite from said humiliation comes when a member of one school of thought on my personality insults the professionalism of a member of the other school of thought, and they fall to bickering.

But there would be no bickering this year. Whartons and Stones all were too riveted, too agog, at the tales told them by Dr. Wharton-Stone about the machinations of Moliere, the gothic email administrator with the alluring female musk.

Elton Stone, the avuncular head of the Stone family (and greatly admired among the Whartons as well), pronounced his diagnosis without reservation. "She wants cunnilingus, son," he said as he loaded his pipe with burley.

The Whartons and the Stones were stationed throughout the house, basement to attic, listening in by means of a system of intercoms installed for the occasion. Elton and I were seated across the table from one another at ground zero—also known as the dining room. On Elton's pronouncement, those close enough for me to hear first gasped, then fell to mumbling, then at last chimed in their agreement. Moliere, they contended, wanted me for more than my camaraderie and wit.

I assured them they were wrong. I stood and denounced them as grobians, but they would not relent.

"The tongue exercises, these so-called 'skidmores'..." said Aunt Ruth Wharton, chief of turpitude at Belverton's Caligula Memorial Psychiatric Center. "She's turning you into her own personal head!"

They all commenced speaking and continued until Elton silenced them with a faux cough.

"She wants cunnilingus-on-demand, son," he said.

Dr. Wharton-Stone touched my hand and looked into my eyes almost lovingly. "It's a known deviance," she said. "You're the victim, here."

"But why?" I asked. "Even if it is a known deviance, why would she want it from me? I'm not particularly handsome, or well-framed, or even charismatic."

"That's what makes it deviant," said Dr. Wharton-Stone's mother in her high, nasal, rarely heard but always charming voice.

Elton turned to me and smiled. "She can read it in your face, son. You're marked."

Instantly a tape recorder appeared in the center of the table. The guests then demanded I volunteer to be regressed into my childhood so they could find the source of my so-called mark—the mark that so attracted Moliere, and which accounted, they claimed, for my inordinate attraction to her musky scent.

After Dr. Wharton-Stone dug her fingernails far enough into the dermis of my arm to raise welts, I agreed.

Serena Stone, Elton's wife, was entrusted with my hypnosis, and a moment later (or so it seemed to me) I was back awake. When I looked about, all of the Whartons and the Stones were staring at me, their faces blanched. Elton's pipe had drooped to his chest and was spilling little brown curls of tobacco onto his green wool sweater. Dr. Wharton-Stone's eyes were teary, and she had to look away when I asked her what was wrong.

Serena rewound the tape and pressed play. This is what I heard.

Serena: Where are you, Barry?

Me: I seem to be out playing with the other lads.

Serena: I mean, where are you on planet Earth?

Me: Why, in Belverton of course. My father is chaplain at Belverton University. I live with him.

Serena: How old are you?

Me: Ten.

Serena: And where is your mother?

Me: I do not remember my mother. After she gave birth to me, we lost track of her. Father says she lost her heart to a bosomy jazz musician named Chiclet.

Serena: All right. A moment ago you said that you were out playing with the lads. What are you lads doing?

Me: We're running past Moo Ridley's door.

Serena: Who is Moo Ridley?

Me: The sister of my father's amanuensis and gal friday, Sal Ridley. The Ridley sisters lived together in our apartment building, directly across the hall from my father and me.

Serena: And why are you running past her door?

Me: We lads were all scared of Moo Ridley. You see it was a fable. A legend. The legend of Moo. And it was not good, my friends. Not good at all, no. The legend had it that Moo once captured a randy film noir instructor from Belverton University. He disappeared, it seemed, right off the planet. Then one day, years later, they found him wandering the quad. He was wearing a Speedo, his body hair had been shaved off, and he could not completely close his jaw.

Serena: Oh my!

The Legend Of Moo Ridley 173

Me: Indeed. We were terrified of her. Terrified. "You have to run past Moo Ridley's door!" my little playmates would shout every day on the way home from school, "or she'll steal your jaw and sell it to Frankenstein!" One day I was being chased by rednecks—

Serena: Rednecks? In Belverton?

Me: Yes, hard to believe, but they all lived together in one house over on Carroll Street. A huge house with three trucks on the lawn and a bony woman who screamed, "Bill, you git yer sticks!" every afternoon at precisely five.

Serena: You get your sticks?

Me: "Git." Trust me. It was "git."

Serena: All right. I want you to go back to that day, the day the rednecks chased you.

Me: I prefer not to.

Serena: You're back there... *now*. Are they chasing you?

Me: Yes!!

Serena: Calm down. It's all in your head. It's not like they're actually going to catch you. Now, why are they chasing you?

Me: While walking past their monstrosity of a home this evening, I spied some sticks and asked the loitering and pit-stained Bill if he was planning to git them.

Serena: Why would they chase you over that?

Me: Oh, my voice was *dripping* with urban sarcasm. Now several lanky men and a so-called "gal" in a red kerchief are running out of the house in overalls and frayed collars. "Git that kid!" the woman screams. The rednecks infesting the lawn are dropping their carburetors and swabbing their faces with oily rags as they begin the chase. Now I'm running as fast as I can to get away from them, throwing my textbooks at them. Oh look! One of the books just struck Bill on the forehead! It's a hardcover atlas but it bounced right off! His head must be made of cobalt!

Serena: So what does this have to do with Moo Ridley?

Me: I am at home now, in the hallway, trying to insert my key into the front door of my apartment. My God! I—the mechanical workings of the loathsome lock are rebuffing the entreaties of my key!

Serena: You mean you can't open the door?

Me: I am pounding against the door, calling for Father, even though I know this is his afternoon to christen children born out of wedlock. What else can I do? "Help! Father! Help! Rednecks!"

Serena: Is Moo Ridley helping you in some way?

Me: Excellent foreshadowing. Indeed, the door to Moo's apartment is opening as the clunking of rural clods echoes ever closer. My God, she is as tall as an Amazon, dressed all in black—black shoes, black sweater, black dress. All the way to the floor...black dress. Her hair is black and short and curled at the ears. Her face is pale. Her mouth smirks. Her eyes beam. Her breasts are enormous. Her waist is wasp thin. Her hips...oh my God, her hips...

Serena: What—what's happening?

Me: She is reaching...she is reaching across the hallway...She has me! Oh my God, Moo Ridley has me! She will steal my jaw and sell it to Frankenstein!

Serena: Settle down. It's just a memory.

Me: We hear...we hear the rednecks. Moo is staring down at me, her red lips grinning and her eyes wild. Oh, if only those rednecks would hurry and save me from Moo Ridley! One of them, a blond, crew-cutted man, is rounding the corner of the hallway! Moo is stuffing me under her skirt! I'm standing there now, in the dark, too scared to—

(A series of sharp sniffs.)

Serena: What's wrong, Barry?

Me: There is a musky odor...it is...it has a strange, calming effect on me. I feel...safe. Secure. For some reason my mouth has begun to water. Wait a minute, the lead redneck is speaking to Moo!

Serena: What is he saying?

Me: He is saying, "Scuse me, ma'am, did you see a little scandazzle runnin' by here?" Wait! What's that sound?!

Serena: What? What is it?

Me: Oh my God, Moo punched the redneck in the jaw with one hand while clutching me to…*herself* with the other!

Serena: Now—

Me: Hush! The other rednecks are talking.

Serena: What are they saying?

Me: "My Sinless Lord and Savior," the woman is saying. "Y'all know who this hyar woman is?"

Serena: Well, do they?

Me: "Whah, this is Moo Ridley," the woman says. The men murmur "Moo." "Don'tcha git it?" the woman is asking them. "She's the one who kidnapped that filmin' war guy and…oh, fer years 'n years, over 'n over…!" The rednecks are quiet. One of them gasps. Another one is gasping. I believe they are hyperventilating. "Mooooo!" they are shouting. "This hyar is that Mooooo woman!" and as they are shouting they are running down the stairs and out of the building.

Serena: What are you doing?

Me: I am tottering. Teetering. Standing, yet reclined in the musk that is Moo. Wait a minute. More footsteps. One set of feet. I...I recognize these steps. It is my father. "Thank you, Moo," I hear him say. Moo is reaching under her dress now and pulling me out. My father is picking me up. "Mea culpa, Barry," he tells me. "I had the locks changed this morning to discourage the impromptu inquiries of the husbands of the ladies I am wont to counsel, and forgot to give you the new key."

Serena: What's Moo doing?

Me: She is grinning at me that wild grin. "See ya round, sonny," she says. My father and I are back in our apartment now. He is turning on the lights. I tell him about the Moo musk. He kneels down in front of me, takes me by the shoulders, and tells me on his honor as a man of God that the musk of Moo is the smell women make when they accidentally swallow their gum. And he is forbidding me to smell it ever again.

Serena: All right, I'm going to count to five...

Dr. Wharton-Stone reached over and pressed the "stop" button. She looked into my eyes. "You need help," she said.
"What I want to know," said my mother-in-law, "is did she see you around? Sonny?"

"No," I replied. "Soon after that adventure she joined the highway patrol and moved to a remote cabin upstate."

"Well," said Elton. "Now we know why you're marked. Now you know why, too."

"With all due respect, Elton, would you please stop saying I'm marked?"

"But you are," he said. "And I'm not speaking metaphorically. I can see it, in low relief on your forehead. A little V."

The Whartons and the Stones hushed as they studied my face.

"It looks like a C from here," said Serena.

They all stared, confused for a moment, then gasped *en masse*.

WHOA
by Desmond Cork—*December 26*

So last week after I called up Nef Snorkjutt I went to meet her at the building where they have the Belverton University Press. See, I called her up and told her about how this dude Bruce was trying to maybe flash nasty with the Babecat? And she said she'd help me track him down.

While I'm walking up to the door of the ol' Press I'm looking around and it's like *really* deserted, cats. And it's winter too and it's cold and there's no lights on. It was Sunday night and not even the morlocks were on duty. I'm thinking what if one of the big computers wakes up to consciousness like in *Star Trek the Movie* and starts thinking things like, "Crap, I'm a computer" and whatnot?

(I have this subscriber thing to that *Wired* magazine so I know about the future, cats.)

Then I see Nef leaning against the rail outside the front door. At first I can't see her because it's night and she's dressed in black and has this long black hair with tiny curls in it like thumbscrews, but she has this face so white it's like a flashlight and when she turned it to me it almost made me squint.

She didn't say anything? But when I got up close she reached over and pinched my cheek. Not really hard though like I saw her do once breaking up a fight between two drunk chicks at Edgar's Café. She smiled and took out these tiny black gloves and put them on only once they were on they didn't look like gloves anymore. They looked more like shiny ink then"Well," she said, "so Lola's *nom de guerre*, well, her *other* name is *Babecat*, is it?"

"That's what I call her," I said. "And the cat's nom de name is *Bruce*."

She pinched my cheek again, a little harder this time. "Let's get a cab, hm?" she said. "You know, a *taxi*."

I followed her out to like the main road in front of the Press building while she dialed up some cab cats on her cell.

"Whoa Nef. You don't have to do that, babe. There's like a cab nasty about a block from here."

"Well, I'm, well…*excellent*."

And she just kept walking ahead of me.

When we got to the cab nasty I told her about we saw this one blue one out front. This dude next to it was filling the cab up with gas and Nef walked up to him and said, "Well, let us, hm, have a ride to 5525 La Boyga Boulevard, shall we?"

He looked at her and spread his eyes wide like a guy would do if he wanted you to know he was surprised but didn't want to say anything because the toothpick might fall out of his mouth. Then a second later he hung up the gas hose on the little hook and took out the toothpick.

"Okay lady," he said. "Let's ride."

"So Nef," I said when we were pulling out onto the road, "What's at this fifty-whatever Sheboyban place?"

"La Boyga," she said. "Why, well, that's where Bruce lives, Desmond."

Whoa. I'm just staring at her 'cause…*whoa*.

"Hey Nef you're like…I mean like how do you know?"

"I know Bruce," she said in a kind of a whisper. "And would you like to know something else, Desmond? I also know the, well, the *Babecat*."

"Whoa..." I say and like I look away from her out my side of the cab and I can sort of see a little of my face in the window 'cause it's dark out but I'm seeing it and I'm thinking, "What's going down? How come I don't know everybody like everybody else does? Are there like meetings and whatnot?" And right then I start thinking that I should read a *lot* more of my mail, cats. And not just email. The stuff they put in the little box downstairs, too.

I turned back to Nef and she was like grinning this evil grin that says she's probably thinking about something metal with a lock in it. I couldn't see her eyes real well except when another car came at us and the lights hit her face. Then you could see her eye whites real good, and the black bull's-eyes were staring right *at* me.

"Jeez, Nef," I said. "It's like you're burning a hole in me."

She turned her head? And looked out her window. "You don't know how much I wish I had that power," she said. Then she goes: "Here we are."

She had the cab dude drive a few houses past this Bruce cat's house and let us out. "We'll sneak up, well, we'll *surprise* them on foot," she said.

"Sweet," I said.

We got out of the ol' cab and it was freezing, cats. Nef paid off the cab dude without asking me to split it, which was pretty cool since I walked out of the apt that night with like a dollar and a stick of gum.

Then the cab pulled away and we started walking toward this Bruce cat's building.

"So Nef, are you going to kick the crap out of ye ol' Bruce?"

"And if I do, what, well, what will *you* be doing? Holding my purse?"

"Okay. But I was thinking once I'm in there? Well, first I'm gonna get warm 'cause it's maybe below freezing out here. You think this Bruce has some rumba brewing?"

"This is his building," she said.

It was one of these short buildings where the bricks look really new and there's a driveway in the front in the shape of a horseshoe for buses and scooters and whatnot. There were lights on at the front door and a doorcat tipping his hat at people.

"Let's walk round back and climb up the fire escape," Nef said.

So that's what we did, cats. This Bruce lived on like the second floor and while we were walking up I could hear a football game from one of the apts. It was muffled 'cause it's winter and the windows are closed in the winter usually. When I looked around to see which one it was I could see it had these white blinds that didn't reach all the way down and you could see this lamp just inside the window that gave off this summery kind of light that shone on the back of this leather sofa that was just screaming for me to jump in for a nap, cats.

There was some other apt that I like couldn't see in? But it was playing one of those VH1 shows about celebs who pretend to be friends and go live in this house where these other cats give them jokes to play on each other then tape them behind this screen calling each other assholes. (VH1 ran out of rock bands to profile around 2001, cats.)

And cookies. You know those sugar cookies that sometimes moms like to bake? They have this smell, am I right? It's a smell that has muscles, cats. Soft muscles that bulge up in your nose holes and hang there.

"Desmond," Nef said while I was thinking about the muscley smell. "Are you, um, *snuffling?*"

"Nope."

"Well, why don't you get up here and eavesdrop with me?"

So I jumped up on the little fire escape landing with her. She was looking in this window from the side and so I stood on the other side and looked in too.

And there was the evidence, cats. I was sort of hoping I was wrong and a big dumb guy that Nef would end up yelling at? But I wasn't. It was a real down too, cats. Because the one thing I wasn't thinking about just before I started thinking about it was that the Babecat might get yearny for some other cat's nasty. But there she was lying on a gym mat panting in her fishnets and garters and not much else.

I figured they hadn't gotten started sweating on each other yet because when I looked in this Bruce was still washing his face. And like what kind of rude cat waits till his date shows up to wash his face? Am I right?

So when he gets done with his face he comes out to the room with the Babecat in it. He's wearing this big flowy t-shirt cats and these little gym shorts and sneakers and then he stands next to the Babecat and starts doing jumping jacks.

"Hey Nef," I whispered, "why is he jumping up and down like that?"

"To wear himself out between, well, *rounds*."

"Why does he have to jump up and down to wear himself out?"

"Because nothing else works."

I was about to say "why" again but Bruce and the Babecat started talking.

"So Lola," said Bruce, "I can't believe the rockdroid fell for the veggie deli story. I mean, that's hittin' the pipe kinda hard, ya know babe?"

"He's not that bad," said the Babecat. "He's really sweet. He's just not...a jackhammer."

And cats, when she said "jackhammer"? She made this look with her face like a kid makes when they see their first card trick.

"Hey..." says this Bruce cat kind of moany-like. "Ya wanna start slammin'?"

"Hey Nef," I asked. "Shouldn't you be kicking Bruce's ass?"

"Shh!" Nef said. "Why don't you watch him? You might, you know, *learn* something."

"You know why I like you?" the Babecat asked Bruce. (I think the whole slamming deal was on hold for a sec.) "I like you because you don't have to wear latex."

"Yep," Bruce said. "Snippety-snip! I had that problem taken care of years ago."

"Didn't it hurt right after?"

"Only when I walked."

They laughed.

"Why do you like *me?*" the Babecat asked.

"Okay babe," he said, "I dig you because you're wild, but without the whips and ropes."

"That's, well," Nef said, "that's...*enough!*"

She banged on the glass almost hard enough to punch through, and the Babecat and Bruce whipped their heads around really fast.

"It's Professor Snorkjutt!" shouted Bruce.

"Oh my God!" the Babecat said. "And Des is with her!"

Nef started getting the window open and it was kind of a race cats, 'cause while she's doing that the Babecat and this Bruce are throwing on all kinds of clothes. When they grabbed their coats and headed for the door? Nef turned around and ran down the fire escape.

"Desmond!" she shouted up to me. "They're getting a, well, *way!* You get in the window and chase them down the stairs and I will...um...I suppose you would say *head them off* in the parking lot!"

"I'm on it babe!" I said.

I got Bruce's window open and climbed in. When I got on my feet in his apt I noticed it was a *lot* warmer in there than it was outside, cats. And I could smell some of the best rumba that I'd ever smelled brewed on this earth or something. So I follow the smell to the kitchen and I look in and there's this full carafe of happening brown rumba. Steaming. The package the brown coffee powder came in was still on the top of the wastebasket.

Whoa. Costa Rica.

And something in my head says, "Des, aren't you supposed to be chasing the Brucecat and Babe?" And I'm like, "Whoa, what did I just think?" and then, "Look Des, it's probably too late to start chasing them now. Next time jump quicker, yeah?" and then the other part of me says, "Yup. Next time we're on it. Where's the rumba cups?"

So I finally find these mugs and pour myself just enough brew to drown myself in if that's what I was really into. I'm sipping this nasty back when I look up and there's good ol' Nef standing in the kitchen doorway.

She's just sort of staring at me and not saying anything. Her eyes are real wide and she's looking at me like she just now noticed I was somebody completely different from the cat she cabbed over with.

"Hey Nef," I say, "how about a cup du rumba?" and I snap up one of the mugs and start to pour for her.

She just kept looking at me for a second and never said yes or no or anything and then she said, "So Desmond, Bruce and Lola, well, they *escaped* in his car. In just a few hours I imagine your Babecat will have been, well, *slammed* at what I think the engineers call a*lternating speeds*."

"Whoa," I said. "Don't you think we should like do something, Nef?"

She smiled this little smile and said: "Yes, well, I don't think they went far. He can't pass five motels with a woman without pulling into one."

Then she pinched my cheek really hard cats, and pulled me all the way down the stairs to the road outside Bruce's house where she flagged down another cab and we got in.

My face hurt for a whole day after that and my girlfriend was off getting what engineers call slammed but all I could think about was the rumba mug I left half full on Bruce's counter. Sometimes I just want to throw on my belt and go back there and finish it.

THE SNAKETAIL BLIMP
by Nefertiti Snorkjutt—*December 31*

Desmond let Bruce escape just as we were about to rescue Lola *again*, so I decided it was time to call in the, um, big guns, you know? The private investigators who cracked the anti-Slappy vote count conspiracy and outed Cindy Goering as a horse-faced traitor. (Well, they outed the traitor part. Her horsey face was already in, um, plain sight.)

"Time to track down a misogynist, boys," I said. They mumbled amongst themselves, seated on the metal chairs in my Belverton basement. Six men, all in black suits with red ties, and one, by the name I believe of Ervin, or maybe Irving, with an ivory-handled pistol strapped to his hip.

"We're gonna go through that guy like crap through a goose!" rasped Ervin (or Irving). "The way the Carthaginians did at Ostium!"

The boys used their connections in the hotel and food-service industries—waiters, waitresses, cleaning ladies, front-desk bastards, managers, hotel dicks, and gardeners—to shut Bruce and the victimized Lola out of all inns, motels, hotels, and toolsheds.

Ervin reported their progress to me. "We're gonna *squeeze* that misogynist bastard! We've got the beds over here and the breakfasts over there and the enemy in the middle! We're gonna hold onto him by the nose and kick him in the ass! We're gonna gut that misogynist bastard on two fronts, the way the Parthians gutted the legions of Publius Crassus!"

"Lovely, Ervin," I said, circling him. "Or is it Irving?"

He did say something, as I recall, but I'm not really sure what it was, because my cell phone rang. It was one of the other hired dicks reporting that he'd found a dumpster rocking in the alley behind the Belverton Improv comedy club.

"Comedians," I told him, "have disgusting kinks."

"Yah, Ms. Snorkjutt," said the caller. He blew smoke into the receiver like he was written by Raymond Chandler. "But I dunno if a comedian could hold his own like this. Citizens on the scene say this thing's been rocking for going on three hours."

"My God..." I said. "It *is* Bruce!"

"Okey," said the dick.

By the time Ervin and I arrived on the scene, the detective who called me and his other four colleagues had surrounded the dumpster and were busy lighting cigarettes *a la noir*.

Across the alley from the Improv is a sloping hill, you know? Not more buildings. The Improv is on the edge of Belverton proper, and across from it is a hill that slopes upward toward the woods.

We got out of the car and I marched up to the dumpster and gave it a good *kick*. The lid opened slightly and two desperate eyes stared out. A moment later I heard the um, the *gasp* I was rather anticipating. Then: "Professor Snorkjutt?"

"That's right, Bruce," I said. "Time to, um, come out. You're, oh, how do you say it? *Surrounded.*"

The lid flew open and the two of them—Lola and Bruce—stood up. The dumpster was, um, not so disgusting. A mattress, a blanket, some incense.

"No garbage?!" Ervin howled. "How the hell did they pull that off?!"

"It's the dumpster for comedian groupies," Bruce said. "I work at the Improv on weekends. It's my job to make sure the refrigerator in here always has a full bottle of Tanqueray."

Right when I was about to tell them to drop the blanket that was hiding their nubile, well, *shame*, there came a sharp whistling. At first it was, well, *far* and *wee*, but it grew in volume until we were all—Bruce, Lola, me, the dicks—covering our ears and, well, *grimacing* like *Shatner*.

"My, well, *God!*" I shouted. I could barely hear my own voice. The sound was, well, it was like a cross between a jet motor revving for takeoff and a nautical whistle.

Then suddenly it stopped.

"Holy crap!" Ervin shouted. He was looking up the sloping hill on the other side of the alley from the Improv. I, well, *wheeled around*, is what I think is usually said, and saw a lone, stocky figure standing at the top of this hill about fifty yards away. A voice boomed out from him. Either he had a microphone with a hidden amplifier or, well, he was a demigod and I had a *lot* of atoning to do *fast*.

"You are all being observed!" the voice boomed. "By me…"

The figure stepped into the moonlight. I could just make out his face. It was—

"By God Almighty!" shouted Ervin, "It's Mickey Snaketail! Look! Fellas! I thought we'd lost him!"

And Ervin was right. It, well, it *was* Mickey Snaketail! I had not seen him since Maui, and then he couldn't speak, or *wouldn't* speak.

"Who…*what* is Mickey Snaketail?" I asked.

"Nobody really knows," said Ervin. "And nobody knows how he can make his voice boom out like that, either, or how he knows just where to stand so the moonlight catches his face when he wants to be recognized."

"I've been summoned…"

It was a young girl's voice. Well, not *too* young, maybe twenty-six. And I noticed, yes, it was the email administrator from the Belverton University Press. Her name is, oh… *Moliere*, hm? Goth girl, I think. She was wearing a t-shirt and very tiny panties and no skirt at all.

"Moliere? Moliere?"

I knew *that* voice. It was Barry Fest, running right behind her, mopping his face with a clump of tulle.

"Excuse me, Moliere," he continued. "That was rather sudden, abrupt, nay, *impulsive*. I believe you nearly crushed my windpipe when you jumped up like that—"

"Pipe down, boss," she said. "I've been summoned by Snake-boy."

Fest looked over at Snaketail.

"Mickey!" he said, "what are you doing out here?"

"You, well, *know* Snaketail?" I asked.

"He's my chaperone," Fest said. "He's been working for my wife."

The Moliere girl giggled. "He wasn't doin' a very good job of it tonight!"

"That's right," Fest said. "Where were you, Mickey? Moliere has…well, there is no other way to put it. She has had her way with…my face!"

"You're welcome," Mickey's voice boomed back.

"Hmm," I said. "In Maui you couldn't talk, Snaketail. What, as they say, is the deal with *that?*"

"Like, what's the deal with what, Nef babe?"

It was Des Cork, picking his way sleepily down the, well, *crowded* alley in his pajamas with the little pirates on them.

"This really loud whistle woke me up and I…whoa…" He was looking at the dumpster. "Babecat," he said to Lola. "Like what are you doing in the trash?"

"Nyuk! Nyuk! Nyuk!"

From the other end of the alley, in a thong and the, well, the *dog collar* I gave him, strutted the barefoot Slappy Goering.

"It was I who emailed Moliere's résumé to the Press," Snaketail's voice boomed out. "It was I who convinced Cindy Goering to sabotage Slappy's presidential campaign. It was I who tattooed the message on Dr. Wharton-Stone's labia seventeen years ago."

"My God, Mickey," said Fest. "How did you do that?"

"Calligraphy pen with a specialty nib," the voice echoed. "And a very small flashlight."

I think it was at that moment, or at some moment near that moment, that we all noticed a large shadow in the sky, moving across the moon. A rope ladder was hurled from this shadow, and its end touched the ground right in front of Mickey.

"Holy crap!" shouted Ervin. "It's the Snaketail blimp!"

Snaketail took hold of the rope ladder and began climbing up.

"Bruce and Lola..." boomed the Snaketail voice, "follow me!"

The two of them hopped out of the dumpster and ran for the ladder.

"Whoa, Babecat," said Des. "You're like leaving? That's harsh, babe."

She stopped for a moment and looked deep into his, well, yes, deep into his eyes. "Oh, Des," she said. "I've always wanted to get on a flying saucer and go to another planet. And this is pretty close!"

By that time, Bruce had already scaled the ladder and was inside the blimp. Now Lola climbed up.

"Slappy Goering!" boomed Snaketail. "Follow me!"

"Snakety!" cried Slappy as he scampered over to the rope ladder.

"Slappy!" I scolded. "You come here and sit!"

He walked over to me and looked deep into my, well, yes, deep into my eyes. "Snakety!" he cried again, and scampered back over to the rope ladder and climbed up while it swung under his weight.

"Moliere!"

The Goth girl ran to the ladder.

"My mom is single and kinky!" she shouted to Fest as she climbed. "Bang her while I'm gone!"

"And you..." Mickey boomed gravely, as he looked up the sloping hill. We followed his eyes to a lone figure just below the tree line. A skirt, short black hair...

"I...oh my God..." said Fest. "It's Moo Ridley!"

The figure approached the ladder.

"Nef," she said as she passed me.

"Moira," I said.

She was no little, well, *girl*, but she hauled herself up that rope ladder like she was Quasimodo riding the bells.

Then Snaketail climbed up after them. And, um, well just before he went inside the blimp he looked back down at us and said, "Farewell, friends, we're off to another dimension!"

And he, well, *disappeared* inside.

The rope ladder lifted off the ground and disappeared into the belly of the blimp, accompanied by a faint *whir* as it did.

Then the blimp began to move. We ran to follow it—me, Des, Barry, and the six dicks—as it floated in the sky down the alley and across the highway that the alley opens onto. On the other side of this highway is a steep drop-off, protected by rails, and in the distance you can see Jasper City in the valley beneath Belverton. It was dark. The lights were on all over Jasper City. It was, well, it was *quite* a beautiful spectacle. And there, in the darkness, floating toward Jasper, was the Snaketail blimp.

"Where do you, um, think the blimp is going, Ervin?" I asked when we reached the rails. "Another dimension? Another country? Snaketail's home town?"

"Nah…" he rasped. "They'll be back. That blimp is going to moor at the Jasper City Radisson for the night. That's as far as they go!"

"How do you know?"

"Snaketail!" Ervin called across space to the blimp. "You beautiful bastard! I read your blog!"

"Well like, what are they going to do there dude?" asked Des.

"I dunno," rasped Ervin. "Orgy?!"

"Barry!" came an officious voice. "Barry!"

We turned around to the highway. There, standing on the median and coming toward us was Fest's wife, Victoria Wharton-Stone.

We ran.

THE END

Made in the USA
Las Vegas, NV
23 April 2021